Puffin Books
Editor: Kaye Webb
Red Fox

'All five puppies were fine specimens of their kind, their woolly puppy coats of a bright rich ruddy tone, their slim little legs very black and clean ... But there was one among them who always came out on top of the scramble ... He was just a trifle larger than any of his fellows: his coat was of a more emphatic red; and in his eyes there was a shade more of that intelligence of glance which means that the brain behind it can reason.' This big brave puppy was Red Fox, and this is the true-to-life story of the life cycle of a fox in the eastern Canadian backwoods.

Red Fox was unusual in many ways: he had great intelligence and strength, and became extremely wise and brave as he learned to outwit his natural enemies in the wilds, the lynxes, the bears, the eagles, a lesson he carefully passed on to his children. He also learned how to outsmart the human hunters who tried, with their guns, hunting dogs and traps, to catch the wily fox who raided their chicken runs and stole the bait from their traps. But even Red Fox could make a mistake, and one day he was captured.

Red Fox is a superb story of adventure and survival, told by one of the greatest naturalists and nature writers. The illustrations, by John Schoenherr, capture the true spirit of the wilderness that was his home.

CHARLES G. D. ROBERTS

RED FOX

Illustrated by John Schoenherr

Introduction by David McCord

Puffin Books

Puffin Books
Penguin Books Ltd,
Harmondsworth, Middlesex, England
Penguin Books, 625 Madison Avenue, New York, New York 10022, U.S.A.
Penguin Books Australia Ltd,
Ringwood, Victoria, Australia
Penguin Books (N.Z.) Ltd,
182–190 Wairau Road, Auckland 10, New Zealand

First published in Great Britain under the Longman Young Books imprint 1974
Published in Puffin Books 1976

Made and printed in Great Britain by
Richard Clay (The Chaucer Press) Ltd,
Bungay, Suffolk
Set in Linotype Baskerville

Contents

Introduction

As one responsible for asking and then urging a publisher to bring out a new edition of *Red Fox* – a once quite famous book, long out of print – it is good that this brief but affectionate tribute to the text is being written by a small boy of nine or ten who keeps telling me what to say. Of course the small boy and I are the same person, but he is still very much alive and he has (far beyond me) all the wisdom, memory, thirst, and unquenchable fire of youth. He likewise has – which seems important – the same translatable love of this animal story as of the time when it lay open in his lap. That was very long ago in the heart of the Pennsylvania Poconos, a lonely upland, winesap region, but in no way so wild or primitive as the New Brunswick, Ringwaak land of *Red Fox* to the north and far, far off to the east. My younger self explains that he had been to Canada when he was six and would go again into those deep woods, or woods much like them, by canoe or afoot a good many times when he grew up.

But before he grew up, he was to live for three years on the edge of a vanishing frontier in southern Oregon close by the swift and sinuous Rogue River, famous for its fishing. And it was his special luck (if I may speak for him) to carry to the Rogue the memory of *Red Fox*, for he didn't own the book. And carry also the memory of dozens of other animal, bird, and insect stories which Sir Charles G. D. Roberts, as he later became, had collected in other remarkable volumes called *The Watchers of the Trails, The Feet of the Furtive, Haunters of the Silences, The Kindred of the Wild,* to name just four. Day by day, the truth of these books unfolded before him in a wilderness of his own.

It should be clear that Sir Charles (I like to call him that, for he was one of the first three Canadians to be knighted) had a magic way with titles. He could charm you right into a book, and the charm did not die when you had entered. The small boy had no need to ask me now – as he did – if that old shiver of delight went up my spine as I was writing down those titles. *The Feet of the Furtive!* Who, I ask, can fail to sense the mystery, the poetry, and the drama in the very order of those words? Just glance at the chapter headings in *Red Fox* itself: 'Some Little People of the Snow', 'The Yellow Thirst', 'A Royal Marauder'.

One might be tempted to begin with 'Some Little People of the Snow', but that would be a grave mistake. This book is much more than a story or a string of episodes. It is a novel about an animal – about many animals, but about a strong, wise, ingenious, and courageous animal in particular. *Red Fox,* I say, while my small prompter's mind is elsewhere, is one of the two finest wild animal stories ever written in English. Few readers of natural history would disagree with me, I believe, when I say that *Tarka the Otter* by Henry Williamson is the other. If *Tarka* (to which I am devoted) is the greater book, the more poetic book, the more ecstatic book, one must also grant at once that the setting is in England, that man enters and exits from the tale at will, that man and dogs are Tarka's constant threat. Red Fox himself, on the other hand, roams through a sparsely settled backwoods country. Man has but small relation even to a few of the chapters. It is purely fox that we are following in his natural wild state – his life as it relates to other wild life, from bear and porcupine to owl and grouse and mouse and weasel. Birds and animals just as they are: no foolish nicknames. A skunk is called a skunk, a rabbit is a rabbit, a lynx is a lynx.

As we pass through the joys and griefs and dangers and rewards of fox and vixen, we pass through spring in the north, where it is swift and glorious in arrival; through summer, splendid fall, and into the intensely cold, almost subarctic winter. One learns the truth of one of the many wise things that Henry Beston has said: 'Summer is the season of motion, winter is the season of form.' Don't forget that.

Perhaps the greatest gift which *Red Fox* can bestow on us in our bewildering time is the sense of dignity with which an animal like a fox or wolf is born. There is no permissiveness in animal youth. Cubs are taught their lessons well and harshly, because if they fail to learn them they will very soon fail to survive. Quite rightly here, there is no glossing over in the author's words or descriptions, though he does not dwell on bloodshed. The defenceless – rabbit and mouse, for example – *are* defenceless. Nature is just as cruel as she is enthralling. We today, the bulk of us, are now so far removed from the wilderness that we do not know what it is like. Cradle of life, it is equally the noble background for death. Our forefathers knew. But to see the natural world from a plane, from a boat with an outboard, or to violate the silence with a snarling snowmobile in the heart of the ancient wood is to miss almost everything. Just to read this book will make you ask yourself: Is man the true creature of dignity, courage, grace, and individual resourcefulness, or is it the better part of the wild populace which he is hastening, one by one, to its extinction?

A rather solemn question to ask at the outset of a thrilling book written by a man who was a respected poet, an accurate observer of nature in the backwoods as he knew it in New Brunswick, a man who never distorts or seems to guess. You trust Red Fox as an animal and as a hero. I say this openly, with my young collaborator who agrees, still knowing, as he does, the final words of the last chapter by heart.

Some years ago I left at the University of New Brunswick – for Charles G. D. Roberts remains one of its most distinguished graduates – these seven words in final tribute:

HE STUDIED HERE TO TESTIFY THE WILDERNESS

David McCord

Preface

In the following story I have tried to trace the career of a fox of the backwoods districts of Eastern Canada. The hero of the story, Red Fox, may be taken as fairly typical, both in his characteristics and in the experiences that befall him, in spite of the fact that he is stronger and cleverer than the average run of foxes. This fact does not detract from his authenticity as a type of his kind. He simply represents the best, in physical and mental development, of which the tribe of the foxes has shown itself capable. In a litter of young foxes there is usually one that is larger and stronger, and of more finely coloured fur, than his fellows. There is not infrequently, also, one that proves to be much more sagacious and adaptable than his fellows. Once in a while such exceptional strength and such exceptional intelligence may be combined in one individual. This combination is apt to result in just such a fox as I have made the hero of my story.

The incidents in the career of this particular fox are not only consistent with the known characteristics and capacities of the fox family, but there is authentic record of them all in the accounts of careful observers. Every one of these experiences has befallen some red fox in the past, and may befall other red foxes in the future. There is no instance of intelligence, adaptability, or foresight given here that is not abundantly attested by the observations of persons who know how to observe accurately. In regard to such points, I have been careful to keep well within the boundaries of fact. As for any emotions which Red Fox may once in a great while seem to display, these may safely be accepted by the most cautious as fox emotions, not as human emotions. In so far as man is himself an animal, he is subject to and impelled by many emotions which he must share with not a few other members of the animal kingdom. Any full presentation of an individual animal of one of the more highly developed species must depict certain emotions not altogether unlike those which a human being might experience under like conditions. To do this is not by any means, as some hasty critics would have it, to ascribe human emotions to the lower animals.

C. G. D. R.
Fredericton, N. B., *August, 1905.*

Red Fox

1 *The Price of His Life*

Two voices, a mellow, bell-like baying and an excited yelping, came in chorus upon the air of the April dawn. The musical and irregularly blended cadence, now swelling, now diminishing, seemed a fit accompaniment to the tender, thin-washed colouring of the landscape which lay spread out under the grey and lilac lights of approaching sunrise. The level country, of mixed woodland and backwoods farm, still showed a few white patches here and there where the snow lingered in the deep hollows; but all over the long, wide southward-facing slope of the uplands, with their rough woods broken by occasional half-cleared, hillocky pastures, the spring was more advanced. Faint green films were beginning to show on the birch and poplar thickets, and over the pasture hillocks; and every maple hung forth a rosy veil that seemed to imitate the flush of morning.

The music of the dogs' voices, melodious though it was, held something sinister in its sweetness – a sort of menacing and implacable joy. As the first notes of it came floating up from the misty lowlands, an old red fox started up from his sleep under a squat juniper-bush on the top of a sunny bank. Wide-awake on the instant, he stood listening critically to the sound. Then he came a few paces down the bank, which was open, dotted with two or three bushes and boulders, and its turf already green through the warmth of its sandy soil. He paused beside the mouth of a burrow which was partly screened by the evergreen branches of a juniper. The next moment another and somewhat smaller fox appeared, emerging briskly from the burrow, and stood beside him, intently listening.

The thrilling clamour grew louder, grew nearer, muffled now and then for a few moments as the trail which the dogs were following led through some dense thicket of spruce or fir. Soon an uneasy look came over the shrewd, greyish-yellow face of the old fox, as he realized that the trail in question was the one which he had himself made but two hours earlier, on his return from a survey of a neighbouring farmer's hen-roost. He had taken many precautions with that homeward trail, tangling and breaking it several times; but he knew that ultimately, for all its deviations and subtleties, it might lead the dogs to this little warm den on the hillside, wherein his mate had but yesterday given birth to five blind, helpless, whimpering puppies. As the slim red mother realized the same fact, her fangs bared themselves in a silent snarl, and, backing up against the mouth of the burrow, she stood there an image of savage resolution, a dangerous adversary for any beast less powerful than bear or panther.

To her mate, however, it was obvious that something more than valour was needed to avert the approaching peril. He knew both the dogs whose chiming voices came up to him so unwelcomely on the sweet spring air. He knew that both were formidable fighters, strong and woodswise. For the sake of those five helpless, sprawling ones at the bottom of the den, the mother must not be allowed to fight. Her death, or even her serious injury, would mean their death. With his sharp ears cocked very straight, one paw lifted alertly, and an expression of confident readiness in his whole attitude, he waited a moment longer, seeking to weigh the exact nearness of the menacing cries. At length a wandering puff of air drawing up from the valley brought the sound startlingly near and clear. Like a flash the fox slipped down the bank and darted into the underbrush, speeding to intercept the enemy.

A couple of hundred yards away from the den in the bank a rivulet, now swollen and noisy with spring rains, ran down the hillside. For a little distance the fox followed its channel, now on one side, now on the other, now springing from rock to rock amid the foamy darting of the waters, now making brief, swift excursions among the border thickets. In this way he made his trail obscure and difficult. Then, at what he held a fitting distance from home, he intersected the line of his old trail, and halted upon it ostentatiously, that the new scent might unmistakably overpower the old.

The baying and yelping chorus was now very close at hand. The fox ran on slowly, up an open vista between the trees, looking over his shoulder to see what the dogs would do on reaching the fresh trail. He had not more than half a minute to wait. Out from a greening poplar thicket burst the dogs, running with noses to the ground. The one in the lead, baying conscientiously, was a heavy-shouldered, flop-eared, much dewlapped dog of a tawny yellow colour, a half-bred foxhound whose cur mother had not obliterated the instincts bequeathed him by his pedigreed and well-trained sire. His companion, who followed at his heels and paid less scrupulous heed to the trail, looking around excitedly every other minute and yelping to relieve his exuberance, was a big black and white mongrel, whose long jaw and wavy coat seemed to indicate a strain of collie blood in his much mixed ancestry.

Arriving at the point where the trail was crossed by the hot, fresh scent, the leader stopped so suddenly that his follower fairly fell over him. For several seconds the noise of their voices was redoubled, as they sniffed wildly at the pungent turf. Then they wheeled, and took up the new trail. The next moment they saw the fox, standing at the edge of a ribbon of spruce woods and looking back at them superciliously. With a new and wilder note in their cries, they dashed forward frantically to seize him. But his white-tipped, feathery brush flickered before their eyes for a fraction of a second, and vanished into the gloom of the spruce wood.

The chase was now full on, the quarry near, and the old trail forgotten. In a savage intoxication, reflected in the wildness of their cries, the dogs tore ahead through brush and thicket, ever farther and farther from that precious den on the hillside. Confident in his strength as well as in his craft, the old fox led them for a couple of miles straight away, chosing the roughest ground, the most difficult gullies, the most tangled bits of underbrush for his course. Fleeter of foot and lighter than his foes, he had no difficulty in keeping ahead of them. But it was not his purpose to distance them or run any risk of discouraging them, lest they should give up and go back to their first venture. He wanted to utterly wear them out, and leave them at last so far from home that, by the time they should be once more ready to go hunting, his old trail leading to the den should be no longer decipherable by eye or nose.

By this time the rim of the sun was above the horizon, mounting into a rose-fringed curtain of tender April clouds, and shooting long beams of rose across the level country. These beams seemed to find vistas ready everywhere, open lines of roadway, or cleared fields, or straight groves, or gleaming river reaches all appearing to converge towards the far-off fount of radiance. Down one of these lanes of pink glory the fox ran in plain sight, looking strangely large and dark in the mystic glow. Very close behind him came the two pursuers, fantastic, leaping, ominous shapes. For several minutes the chase fled on into the eye of the morning, then vanished down an unseen cross-corridor of the woods.

And now it seemed to the brave and crafty old fox, a very Odysseus of his kind for valour and guile, that he had led the enemy almost far enough from home. It was time to play with them a little. Lengthening out his stride till he had secured a safer lead, he described two or three short circles, and then ran on more slowly. His pursuers were quite out of sight, hidden by the trees and bushes; but he knew very well by his hearing just when they ran into those confusing loops in the trail. As the sudden, excited confusion in their cries reached him, he paused and looked back, with his greyish-ruddy head cocked to one side; and, if laughter had been one of the many vulpine accomplishments, he certainly would have laughed at that moment. But presently the voices showed him that their owners had successfully straightened out the little snarl and were once more after him. So once more he ran on, devising further shifts.

Coming now to a rocky brook of some width, the fox stepped out upon the stones, then leaped back upon his own trail, ran a few steps along it, and finally jumped aside as far as he could, alighting upon a log in the heart of a patch of blueberry scrub. Slipping down from the log, he raced back a little way parallel with his tracks and lay down on the top of a dry hillock to rest. A drooping screen of hemlock branches here gave him effective hiding, while his sharp eyes commanded the brookside and perhaps a hundred yards of the back trail.

In a moment or two, the dogs rushed by, their tongues hanging far out, but their voices still eager and fierce. Not thirty yards away the old fox watched them cynically, wrinkling his narrow nose with aversion as the light breeze brought him their scent. As he watched, the pupils of his eyes contracted to narrow, upright slits of liquid black, then rounded out again as anger yielded to interest. It filled him with interest, indeed, to watch the frantic bewilderment and haste of his pursuers when the broken trail at the edge of the brook baffled them. First they went splashing across to the other bank, and rushed up and down, sniffing savagely for the scent. Next they returned to the near bank and repeated the same tactics. Then they seemed to conclude that the fugitive had attempted to cover his tracks by travelling in the water, so they traced the water's edge exactly, on both sides, for about fifty yards up and down. Finally they returned to the point where the trail was broken, and silently began to work around it in widening circles. At last the yellow half-breed gave voice. He had recaptured the scent on the log in the blueberry patch. As the noisy chorus rose again upon the morning air, the old fox got up, stretched himself somewhat contemptuously, and stood out in plain view with a shrill bark of defiance. Joyously the dogs accepted the challenge and hurled themselves forward; but in the same instant the fox vanished, leaving behind him a streak of pungent, musky scent that clung in the bushes and on the air.

And now for an hour the eager dogs found themselves continually overrunning or losing the trail. More than half their time and energy were spent in solving the riddles which their quarry kept propounding to them. Once they lost fully ten minutes racing up and down and round and round a hillocky sheep-pasture, utterly baffled, while the fox, hidden in the cleft of rock on the other side of the fence, lay comfortably eyeing their performances. The sheep, huddling in a frightened mass in one corner of the pasture, scared by the noise, had given him just the chance he wanted. Leaping lightly upon the nearest, he had run over the thick-fleeced backs of the whole flock, and gained the top of the rail fence, from which he had sprung easily to the cleft in the rock. To the dogs it was as if their quarry had suddenly grown wings and soared into the air. The chase would have ended there but for the mischance of the shifting of the wind. The light breeze which had been drawing up from the south-west all at once, without warning, veered over to the east; and with it came a musky whiff which told the puzzled dogs the whole story. As they raced joyously and clamorously towards the fence, the fox slipped down the other side of the rock and fled away.

A fox's wits are full of resource, and he seldom cares to practice all his accomplishments in one run. But this was a unique occasion; and this fox was determined to make his work complete and thoroughly dishearten his pursuers. He now conceived a stratagem which might, possibly, prove discouraging. Minutely familiar with every inch of his range, he remembered a certain deep deadwater on the brook, bridged by a fallen sapling. The sapling was now old and partly rotted away. He had crossed it often, using it as a bridge for his convenience; and he had noticed just a day or two ago that it was growing very insecure. He would see if it was yet sufficiently insecure to serve his purpose.

Without any more circlings and twistings, he led the way straight to the deadwater, leaving a clear trail. The tree was still there. It seemed to yield, almost imperceptibly, as he leaned upon it. His shrewd and practised perceptions told him that its strength would just suffice to carry him across, but no more. Lightly and swiftly, and not without some apprehension (for he loathed a wetting), he ran over, and halted behind a bush to see what would happen.

Arrived at the fallen tree, the dogs did not hesitate. The trail crossed. They would go where it went. But the tree had something to say in the matter. As the double weight sprang up it, it sagged ominously, but the excited hunters were in no mood to heed the warning. The next moment it broke in the middle with a punky, crumbling sound; and the dogs plunged, splashing and yelping, into the middle of the icy stream.

If the fox, however, had imagined that this unexpected bath would be cold enough to chill the ardour of his pursuers, he was speedily disillusioned. Neither dog seemed to have his attention for one single moment distracted by the incident. Both swam hurriedly to land, scrambled up the bank, and at once resumed the trail. The fox was already well away through the underbrush.

By this time he was tired of playing tricks. He made up his mind to lead the enemy straight, distance them completely, and lose them in the rocky wilderness on the other side of the hill, where their feet would soon get sore on the sharp stones. Then he could rest awhile in safety, and later in the day return by a devious route to the den in the bank and his slim red mate. The plan was a good one, and in all ways feasible. But the capricious fate of the woodfolk chose to intervene.

It chanced that, as the fox passed down an old, mossy wood-road, running easily and with the whole game well in hand, a young farmer carrying a gun was approaching along a highway which intersected the wood-road. Being on the way to a chain of shallow ponds along the foot of the uplands, he had his gun loaded with duck shot, and was unprepared for larger game. The voices of the dogs – now much subdued by weariness and reduced to an occasional burst of staccato clamour – gave him warning of what was afoot. His eyes sparkled with interest, and he reached for his pocket to get a cartridge of heavier shot. But just as he did so the fox appeared.

There was no time to change cartridges. The range was long for BB, but the young farmer was a good shot and had confidence in his weapon. Like a flash he lifted his gun and fired. As the heavy report went banging and flapping among the hills, and the smoke blew aside, he saw the fox dart lightly into the bushes on the other side of the way, apparently untouched. With a curse, devoted impartially to his weapon and his marksmanship, he ran forward and carefully examined the tracks. There was no smallest sign of blood. 'Clean miss, by gum!' he ejaculated; and strode on without further delay. He knew the dogs could never overtake that seasoned old fox. They might waste their time, if they cared to. He would not. They crossed the road just as he disappeared around the next turning.

But the fox, though he had vanished from view so nonchalantly and swiftly, had not escaped unscathed. With the report, he had felt a sudden burning anguish, as of a white-hot needle-thrust, go through his loins. One stray shot had found its mark; and now, as he ran, fierce pains racked him, and every breath seemed to cut. Slower and slower he went, his hind legs reluctant to stretch out in the stride, and utterly refusing to propel him with their old springy force. Nearer and nearer came the cries of the dogs, till presently he realized that he could run no farther. At the foot of a big granite rock he stopped, and turned, and waited, with bare, dangerous fangs gleaming from his narrow jaws.

The dogs were within a dozen yards of him before

they saw him, so still he stood. This was what they had come to seek; yet now, so menacing were his looks and attitude, they stopped short. It was one thing to catch a fugitive in flight. It was quite another to grapple with a desperate and cunning foe at bay. The old fox knew that fate had come upon him at last. But there was no coward nerve in his lithe body, and the uncomprehended anguish that gripped his vitals added rage to his courage. The dogs rightly held him dangerous, though his weight and stature were scarcely half what either of them could boast.

Their hesitation, however, was but momentary. Together they flung themselves upon him, to get lightning slashes, almost simultaneously, on neck and jaw. Both yelped angrily, and bit wildly, but found it impossible to hold down their twisting foe, who fought in silence and seemed to have the strength and irrepressibility of steel springs in his slender body. Presently his teeth met through the joint of the hound's fore paw, and the hound, with a shrill *ki yi*, jumped backward from the fight. But the black and white mongrel was of better grit. Though one eye was filled with blood, and one ear slit to the base, he had no thought of shirking the punishment. Just as the yelping hound withdrew from the mix-up, his long, powerful jaws secured a fair grip on the fox's throat, just back of the jawbone. There was a moment of breathless, muffled, savage growling, of vehement and vindictive shaking. Then the valorous red body straightened itself out at the foot of the rock, and made no more resistance as the victors mauled and tore it. At a price, the little family in the burrow had been saved.

2 *The Lessons of the Wild*

NIGHT after night, for several weeks, the high, shrill barking of a she fox was heard persistently along the lonely ridges of the hills. The mother fox was sorrowing for her mate. When he came no more to the den, she waited till night, then followed the broad, mingled trail of the chase till she found out all that had happened. She was too busy, however – too much driven by the necessities of those five blind sprawlers in the musky depths of the burrow – to have much time for mourning. But when the softly chill spring night lay quiet about her hunting, her loneliness would now and then find voice.

Her hunting was now carried on with the utmost caution. For a time, while her puppies were still blind, she lay in her den all day long, nursing them, and never stirring abroad till the piping of the frogs in the valley pools proclaimed the approach of twilight. Then she would mount the hill and descend into the next valley before beginning to hunt. She would take every precaution to disguise her tracks while in the neighbourhood of her den. Wherever possible, she would steal through the pungent-scented, prickly dwarf-juniper bushes, whose smell disguised her own strong scent, and whose obstinate sharpness was a deterrent to meddlesome and inquisitive noses. Not until she had passed through a belt of particularly rough, stony ground near the top of the hill would she allow her attention to be absorbed in the engrossing labours of the hunt.

Once in what she held a safe region, however, she flung her precautions aside and hunted vehemently. The cubs as yet being entirely dependent upon her milk, it was her first care that she herself should be well fed. Her chief dependence was the wood-mice, whose tiny squeaks she could detect at an astonishing distance. Next in abundance and availability to these were the rabbits, whom she would lie in wait for and pounce upon as they went by. Once in a while an unwary partridge afforded her the relish of variety; and once in a while, descending to the marshy pools, she was cunning and swift enough to capture a wild duck. But the best and easiest foraging of all was that which, just now when she most needed it, she least dared to allow herself. The hens, and ducks, and geese, and turkeys of the scattered backwoods farms were now, with the sweet fever of spring in their veins, vagrant and careless. But while she had the little ones to consider, she would not risk drawing to herself the dangerous attention of men. She did permit herself the luxury of a fat goose from a farmyard five miles away in the other valley. And a couple of pullets she let herself pick up at another farm half a mile beyond. But in her own valley, within a couple of miles of her lair, all the poultry were safe from tooth of hers. She would pass a flock of waddling ducks, near home, without condescending to notice their attractions. Notoriety, in her own neighbourhood, was the last thing she desired. She had no wish to advertise herself.

Thanks to this wise caution, the slim red mother saw no menace approach her den, and went on cherishing her little ones in peace. For a time she heard no more of that ominous hunting music down in the plain, for the hound's well-bitten joint was long in healing. He could not hunt for the soreness of it; and the black and white mongrel did not care to hunt alone, or lacked the expertness to follow the scent. When at length the baying and barking chorus once more came floating softly up to her retreat, somewhat muffled now by the young leafage which had burst out greenly over the hillside, she was not greatly disturbed. She knew it was no trail of hers that they were sniffing out. But she came to the door of her den, nevertheless, and peered forth. Then she emerged altogether, and stood listening with an air of intense hostility, untouched by the philosophic, half-derisive interest which had been the attitude of her slaughtered mate. As she stood there with bared fangs and green-glinting, narrowed gaze, a little group of pointed noses and inquiring ears and keen, mischievous, innocently shrewd eyes appeared in the doorway of the den behind her. The sound was a novel one to them. But their mother's attitude showed plainly that it was also a dangerous and hateful sound, so they stayed where they were instead of coming out to make investigations. Thus early in their lives did they hear that music which is the voice of doom to so many foxes.

As spring ripened towards summer over the warm lowlands and windy uplands, and the aerial blue tones of far-off Ringwaak deepened to rich purples with the deepening of the leafage, the little foxes spent more and more of their time outside the door of their den, and took a daily widening interest in the wonderful, radiant, outer world. Though they little knew it, they were now entering the school of life, and taking their first lessons from the inexorable instructress, Nature. Being of keen wits and restless curiosity, they were to be counted, of course, among Nature's best pupils, marked out for much learning and little castigation. Yet even for them there was discipline in store, to teach them how sternly Nature exacts a rigid observance of her rules.

In mornings, as soon as the sun shone warm upon the face of the bank, the mother would come forth, still sluggish from her night's hunting, and stretch herself out luxuriously on the dry turf a few paces below the mouth of the den. Then would come the cubs, peering forth cautiously before adventuring into the great world. As the mother lay there at full length, neck and legs extended and white-furred belly turned up to the warmth, the cubs would begin by hurling themselves upon her with a chorus of shrill, baby barking. They would nip and maul and worry her till patience was no longer a virtue; whereupon she would shake them off, spring to her feet with a faint mutter of warning, and lie down again in another place. This action the puppies usually accepted as a sign that their mother did not want to play any more. Then there would be, for some minutes, a mad scuffle and scramble among themselves, with mock rages and infantile snarlings, till one would emerge on top of the rolling heap, apparently victor. Upon this, as if by mutual consent, the bunch would scatter, some to lie down with lolling tongues and rest, and some to set about an investigation of the problems of this entertaining world.

All five of these brisk puppies were fine specimens of their kind, their woolly puppy coats of a bright rich ruddy tone, their slim little legs very black and clean, their noses alertly inquisitive to catch everything that went on, their pale yellow eyes bright with all the crafty sagacity of their race. But there was one among them who always came out on top of the scramble; and who, when the scramble was over, always had something so interesting to do that he had no time to lie down and rest. He was just a trifle larger than any of his fellows; his coat was a more emphatic red; and in his eyes there was a shade more of that intelligence of glance which means that the brain behind it can reason. It was he who first discovered the delight of catching beetles and crickets for himself among the grass stems, while the others waited for their mother to show them how. It was he who was always the keenest in capturing the mice and shrews which the mother would bring in alive for her little ones to practise their craft upon. And he it was alone of all the litter who learned how to stalk a mouse without any teaching from his mother, detecting the tiny squeak as it sounded from under a log fifty feet or more from the den, and creeping up upon it with patient stealth, and lying in wait for long minutes absolutely motionless, and finally springing triumphantly upon the tiny, soft, grey victim. He seemed to inherit with special fulness and effectiveness that endowment of ancestral knowledge which goes by the name of instinct. But at the same time he was peculiarly apt in learning from his mother, who was tireless in teaching her puppies, to the best of her ability, whatever it behooved small foxes to know and believe.

At this stage in their development she brought in the widest variety of game, large and small, familiarizing the puppies with the varied resources of the forest. But large game, such as rabbits and woodchucks, she brought in dead, because a live rabbit might escape by one of its wild leaps, and a woodchuck, plucky to the last gasp and armed with formidable teeth, might kill one of its baby tormentors. Partridges, too, and poultry, and all strong-winged and adult birds, she brought in with necks securely broken, lest they should escape by timely flight. It was only young birds and very small animals that were allowed the privilege of helping along the education of the red fox litter.

One day she brought in a black snake, holding its head in her mouth uncrushed, while its rusty, writhing body twined about her head and neck. At her low call the cubs came tumbling eagerly from the burrow, wondering what new game she had for them. But at the sight of the snake they recoiled in alarm. At least, they all but one recoiled. The reddest and largest of the family rushed with a baby growl to his mother's assistance, and tried to tear the writhing coils from her neck. It was a vain effort, of course. But when the old fox, with the aid of her fore paws, wrenched herself free and slapped the trailing length upon the ground, the puppy flung himself upon it without a sign of fear and arrested its attempt at flight. In an instant its tense coils were wrapped about him. He gave a startled yelp, while the rest of the litter backed yet farther off in their dismay. But the next moment,

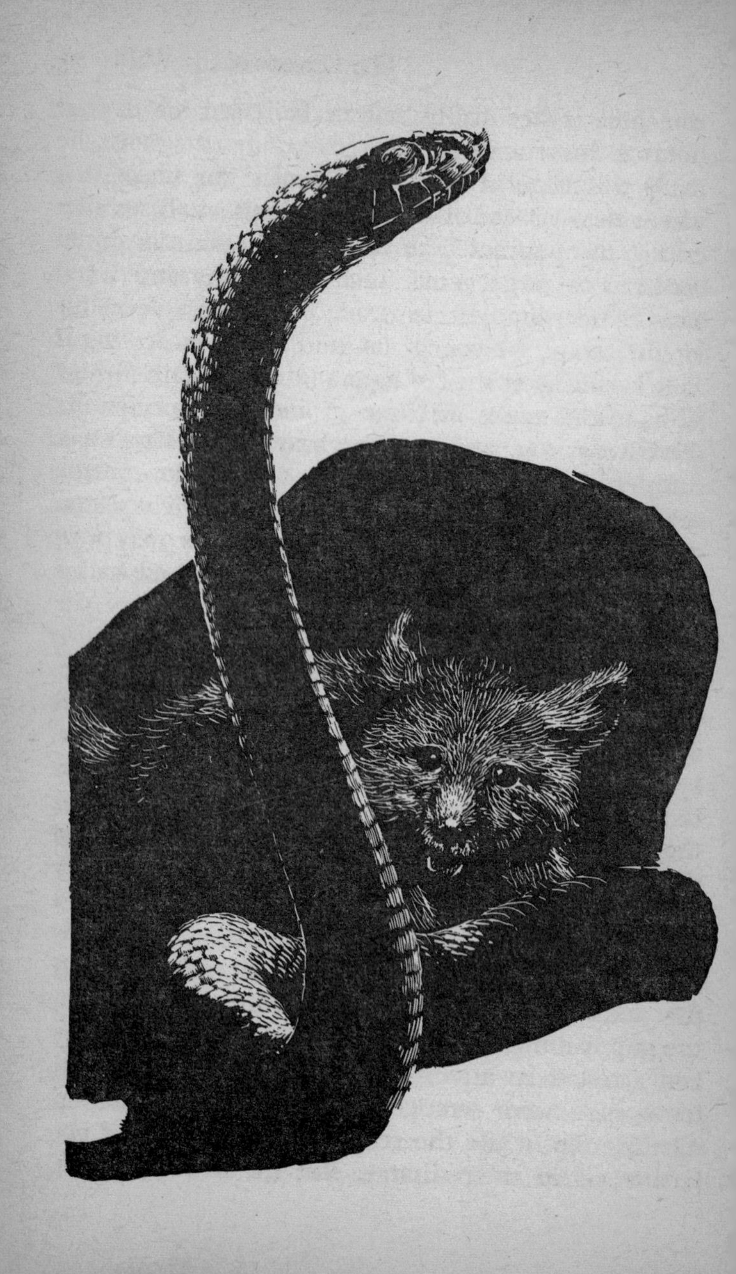

remembering probably how he had seen his mother holding this strange and unmanageable antagonist, he made a successful snap and caught the snake just where the neck joined the head. One savage, nervous crunch of his needle-like young teeth, and the spinal cord was cleanly severed. The tense coils relaxed, fell away. And proudly setting both fore paws upon his victim's body, the young conqueror fell to worrying it as if it had been a mere mouse. He had learned how to handle a snake of the non-poisonous species. As there were no rattlers or copperheads in the Ringwaak country, that was really all he needed to know on the subject of snakes. Emboldened by his easy victory, and seeing that the victim showed no sign of life except in its twitching tail, the other four youngsters now took a hand in the game, till there was nothing left of the snake but scattered fragments.

As the young foxes grew in strength and enterprise, life became more exciting for them. The mother still did her hunting by night, and still rested by day, keeping the youngsters still close about the door of the burrow. In her absence they kept scrupulously out of sight, and silent; but while she was there basking in the sun, ready to repel any dangerous intruder, they felt safe to roam a little, along the top of the bank and in the fringes of the thickets.

One day towards noon, when the sky was clear and the shadows of the leaves lay small and sharp, a strange, vast shadow sailed swiftly over the face of the bank, and seemed to hover for an instant. The old fox leaped to her feet with a quick note of warning. The big red puppy, superior to his brothers and sisters in caution no less than in courage, shot like a flash under the shelter of a thick juniper-bush. The others crouched where they happened to be and looked up in a kind of panic. In what seemed the same instant there was a low but terrible rushing sound overhead, and the great shadow seemed to fall out of the sky. One of the little foxes was just on top of the bank, crouching flat, and staring upwards in terrified amazement. The mother, well understanding the fate that impended, sprang towards him with a screeching howl, hoping to frighten away the marauder. But the great goshawk was not one to be scared by noise. There was a light blow, a throttled yelp, a sudden soundless spread of wide wings, then a heavy flapping; and just as the frantic mother arrived upon the spot the huge bird sprang into the air, bearing a little, limp, red form in the clutch of his talons. When he was gone the rest of the puppies ran shivering to their mother – all but the Red Fox himself, who continued to stare thoughtfully from the covert of his juniper-bush for some minutes. For a long time after that experience he never failed to keep a sharp watch upon the vast blue spaces overhead, which looked so harmless, yet held such appalling shapes of doom.

It was not long after this event, and before the mother had begun to take her young ones abroad upon the serious business of hunting, that the Fate of the wood kindreds struck again at the family of the burrow. It was just in the most sleepy hour of noon. The old fox, with one of the puppies stretched out beside her, was dozing under a bush some distance down the bank. Two others were digging fiercely in a sandy spot on top of the bank, where they imagined perhaps, or merely pretended to imagine, some choice titbit had been buried. A few paces away Red Fox himself, busy, and following his own independent whim as usual, was intent upon stalking some small creature, mouse or beetle or cricket, which had set a certain tuft of grains twitching conspicuously. Some live thing, he knew, was in that tuft of grains. He would catch it, anyway; and if it was good to eat he would eat it.

Closer and closer he crept, soundless in movement as a spot of light. He was just within pouncing distance, just about to make his pounce and pin down the unseen quarry, when a thrill of warning ran through him. He turned his head – but fortunately for him he did not wait to see what danger threatened him. Being of that keen temperament which can act as swiftly as it can think, even as he was turning his head he made a violent lightning-swift leap straight down the bank, towards his mother's side. At the same instant he had a vision of a ghostly grey, crouching, shadowy form with wide green eyes glaring upon him from the embankment. The very next moment a big lynx came down upon the spot which he had just left.

Startled from their work of digging in the sand, the two puppies looked up in wonder. They saw their enterprising brother rolling over and over down the bank. They saw their mother leaping towards them with a fierce cry. They sprang apart, with that sound impulse to scatter which Nature gives to her weak children. Then upon one of them a big muffled paw, armed with claws like steel, came down irresistibly, crushing out the small, eager life. He was snatched up by a pair of strong jaws; and the lynx went bounding away lightly over the bushes with his prize. Finding himself savagely pursued by the mother fox, he ran up the nearest tree, a spreading hemlock, and crouched in the crotch of a limb with his victim under one paw. As the mother circled round and round below, springing up against the trunk in voiceless rage, the lynx glared down on her with vindictive hissings and snarlings. He was really more than a match for her, both in weight and weapons; but he had no desire for a battle with her mother-fury. For perhaps ten minutes she raged against the base of the impregnable trunk. Then realizing her impotence, she turned resolutely away and went back to her three remaining little ones.

For some days now the fox family was particularly cautious. They kept close beside their mother all the time, trembling lest the flame-eyed terror should come back.

Among the wild kindreds, however, an experience of this sort is soon forgotten, in a way. Its lesson remains, indeed, but the shock, the panic fear, fades out. In a little while the green summer world of the hillside was as happy and secure as ever to the fox family, except that a more cunning caution, now grown instinctive and habitual, was carried into their play as into their work.

Work, in fact, now began to enter the lives of the three little foxes, work which to them had all the zest of play. Their mother began to take them hunting with her, in the moonlight or the twilight. They learned to lie in wait beside the glimmering runways, and pounce unerringly upon the rabbit leaping by. They learned to steal up and catch the brooding partridge, which was a task to try the stealth of the craftiest stalker. They learned to trace the grassy galleries of the meadow mice, and locate the hidden scurriers by their squeaks and faint rustlings. And they learned to relish the sweet wild fruits and berries beginning to ripen in the valleys and on the slopes. The youngsters were now losing the woolly baby look of their fur, and beginning to show a desire of independence which kept their mother busy watching lest they should get themselves into mischief. With their independence came some unruliness and overconfidence, natural enough in men or foxes when they first begin to realize their powers. But of the three, Red Fox, who surpassed his brother and sister no less in stature and intelligence than in the vivid colouring of his young coat, was by far the least unruly. It was no small part of his intelligence that he knew how much better his mother knew than he. When she signalled danger, or caution, or watchfulness, he was all attention instantly to find out what was expected of him; while the other two were sometimes wilful and scatter-brained. Taking it all in all, however, the little family was harmonious and contented, and managed for all its tragedies, to get an immense amount of fun out of its life in the warm summer world.

3 *Black Marks and Birchings*

Now came the critical time when the young foxes showed a disposition to wander off and hunt by themselves; and at this stage of his education Red Fox, whose quickness had hitherto saved him from any sharp discipline in the school of Nature, came under the ferule more than once. Instinct could not teach him everything. His mother was somewhat overbusy with the other members of the family, who had shown themselves so much more in need of her care. And so it came about that he had to take some lessons from that rude teacher, experience.

The first of these lessons was about bumblebees. One afternoon, while he was hunting field-mice in a little meadowy pocket half-way up the hillside, his eager nose caught the scent of something much more delicious and enticing in its savour than mice. It was a smell of warmth and sweetness, with a pungent tang; and instinct assured him confidently that anything with a smell like that must be very good to eat. What instinct forgot to suggest, however, was that anything so delectable was likely to be expensive or hard to get. It is possible (though some say otherwise!) to expect too much of instinct.

Field-mice utterly forgotten, his mouth watering with expectation, the young fox went sniffing hungrily over the turf, following the vague allurement hither and thither, till suddenly it steamed up hot and rich directly under his nose. A big black and yellow bumblebee boomed heavily past his ears, but he was too busy to notice it. His slim pink tongue lolling out with eagerness, he fell to digging with all his might, heedless of the angry, squeaking buzz which straight away began under his paws.

The turf over the little cluster of comb was very thin. In a moment those busy paws had penetrated it. Greedily Red Fox thrust his nose into the mass of bees and honey. One taste of the honey, enchantingly sweet, he got. Then it seemed as if hot thorns were being hammered into his nose. He jumped backwards with a yelp of pain and astonishment; as he did so the bees came swarming about his eyes and ears, stinging furiously. He ran for his life, blindly, and plunged into the nearest clumps of juniper. It was the best thing he could do, for the stiff twigs brushed off those bees which were clinging to him, and the rest, like all of their kind, hated to take their delicate wings into the tangle of the branches. They hummed and buzzed angrily for a while outside the enemy's retreat, then boomed away to repair the damage to their dwelling. Within his shelter, meanwhile, the young fox had been grovelling with hot anguish, scratching up the cool, fresh earth and burying his face in it. In a few minutes, finding this remedy insufficient, he crept forth and slunk miserably down to the brook, where he could rub his nose and eyes, his whole tormented head, indeed, in a chilly and healing mess of mud. There was no better remedy in existence for such a hurt as his, and soon the fever of the stings was so far allayed that he remembered to go home. But he carried with him so strangely disfigured a countenance that the rest of the family regarded him with disapproval, and he felt himself an outcast.

For nearly two days Red Fox stayed at home, moping in the dark of the burrow, and fasting. Then his clean young blood purged itself of the acrid poison, and he came forth very hungry and bad-tempered. It was this bad temper, and the recklessness of his unwonted hunger, that procured him the second taste of Nature's discipline.

It was late in the afternoon, and the rest of the family were not yet ready to go a-hunting, so he prowled off by himself to look for a rabbit. His appetite was quite too large to think of being satisfied with mice. About a hundred yards above the den, as he crept stealthily through the underbrush, he saw a black and white striped animal moving sluggishly down a cattle path. It did not look at all formidable, yet it had an air of fearlessness which at any other time or in any other mood would have made so shrewd a youngster as Red Fox stop and think. Just now, however, he was in no sort of humour to stop and think. He crouched, tense with anticipation; waited till he could not wait another second; then bounded forth from his hiding-place, and flung himself upon the deliberate stranger.

Red Fox, as we have seen, was extraordinarily quick. In this case his rush was so quick that he almost caught the stranger unawares. His jaws were almost about to snap upon the back of that striped neck. But just before they could achieve this an astounding thing happened. The stranger whirled as if for flight. His tail went up in the air with a curious jerk. And straight in his eyes and nose and mouth Red Fox received a volley of something that seemed to slap and blind and choke him, all three at once. His eyes felt as if they were burnt out of his head. At the same time an overpowering, strangling smell clutched his windpipe and seemed almost to close up his throat in a paroxysm of repulsion. Gasping desperately, sputtering and staggering, the unhappy youngster rushed away, only to throw himself down and grovel wildly in the moss and leaves, coughing, tearing at mouth and eyes with frantic paws, struggling to rid himself of the hideous, throttling, slimy thing. And the skunk, not turning to bestow even one scornful glance upon his demoralized assailant, went strolling on indifferently down the cow-path, unafraid of the world. As for Red Fox, it was many minutes before he could breathe without spasms. For a long time he rolled in the leaves and moss, scrubbing his face fiercely, getting up every minute and changing his place, till all the ground for yards about was impregnated with skunk. Then he betook himself to a mound of dusty soil, and there repeated his dry ablutions till his face was so far cleansed that he could breathe without choking, and his scalded eyes were once more of some use to see with. This accomplished, he went sheepishly home to the burrow – to be received this time with disgust and utter reprobation. His mother stood obstinately in the doorway and snarled him an unequivocal denial. Humiliated and heartsore, he was forced to betake himself to the hollow under the juniper-bush above the den, where his valiant father had slept before him. Not for three unhappy days was he allowed to enter the home den, or even come very close to the rest of the family. Even then an unprejudiced judge would have felt constrained to declare that he was anything but sweet. But it really takes a very bad smell to incommode a fox.

During the days when the curse of the skunk still lay heavy upon him, he found that his adversity, like most others, had its use. His hunting became distinctly easier, for the small wild creatures were deceived by his scent. They knew that a skunk was always slow in movement, and therefore they were very ready to let this unseen hunter, whose smell was the smell of a skunk, come within easy springing distance. In this way, indeed, Red Fox had his revenge for the grievous discomfiture which he had suffered. For presently, it seemed, word went abroad through the woods that some skunks were swift of foot and terrible of spring as a wildcat; and thenceforth all skunks of the Ringwaak country found the chase made more difficult for them.

In the meantime, the mother fox was beginning to get very nervous because two of her litter were inclined to go foraging in the neighbourhood of the farmhouse in the valleys. In some way, partly by example and partly no doubt by a simple language whose subtleties evade human observation, she had striven to impress upon them the suicidal folly of interfering with the man-people's possessions. Easy hunting, she conveyed to them, was not always good hunting. These instructions had their effect upon the sagacious brain of Red Fox. But to his brother and sister they seemed stupid. What were ducks and chickens for if not to feed foxes; and what were farmers for if not to serve the needs of foxes by providing chickens and ducks? Seeing the trend of her offspring's inclinations, the wise old mother made up her mind to forsake the dangerous neighbourhood of the den and lead her little family farther back into the woods, out of temptation. Before she had quite convinced herself, however, of the necessity of this move, the point was very roughly decided for her – and Red Fox received another salutary lesson.

It came about in this way. One afternoon, a little before sundown, Red Fox was sitting on a knoll overlooking the nearest farmyard, taking note of the ways of men and of the creatures dependent upon men. He sat up on his haunches like a dog, his head to one side, his tongue showing between his half-open jaws, the picture of interested attention. He saw two men working in the field just behind the little grey house. He saw the big black and white mongrel romping in the sunny, chip-strewn yard with the yellow half-breed, who had come over from a neighbouring farm to visit him. He saw a flock of fat and lazy ducks paddling in the horse-pond behind the barn. He saw, also, a flock of half-grown chickens foraging carelessly for grass hoppers along the edge of the hay-field, and thought wistfully what easy game they would be for even the most blundering of foxes. In a vague way he made up his mind to study the man people very carefully, in order that he might learn to make use of them without too great risk.

As he watched, he caught sight of a small red shape creeping stealthily through the underbrush near the hay-field. It was his heedless brother; and plainly he was stalking those chickens. Red Fox shifted uneasily, frightened at the audacity of the thing, but sympathetically interested all the same. Suddenly there was a rush and a pounce, and the small red shape landed in the midst of the flock. The next moment it darted back into the underbrush, with a flapping chicken swung over its shoulder; while the rest of the flock, squawking wildly with terror, fled headlong towards the farmyard.

At the sudden outcry, the dogs in the yard stopped playing and the men in the field looked up from their work.

'That's one o' them blame foxes, or I'll be jiggered!' exclaimed one of the men, the farmer–woodsman named Jabe Smith, whose knowledge of wilderness lore had taught him the particular note of alarm which fowls give on the approach of a fox. 'We'll make him pay dear for that chicken, if he's got one!' And the two hurried up towards the house, whistling for the dogs. The dogs came bounding towards them eagerly, well knowing what fun was afoot. The men got their guns from the kitchen and led the dogs across the hay-field to the spot where the chickens had been feeding. In five minutes the robber's trail was picked up, and the dogs were in full cry upon it. Red Fox, watching from his knoll behind the house, cocked his ears as the musical but ominous chorus arose on the sultry air; but he knew it was not he the dogs were hunting, so he could listen more or less philosophically.

The reckless youngster who had stolen the chicken was terrified by the outcry which he had excited at his heels; but he was plucky and kept hold of his prize, and headed straight for the den, never stopping to think that this was one of the deadliest sins on the whole of the fox kins' calendar. Running for speed only, and making no attempt at disguising his trail, he was nevertheless lucky enough to traverse a piece of stony ground where the trail refused to lie, and then to cross the brook at a point where it was wide and shallow. Here the pursuers found themselves completely at fault. For a time they circled hither and thither, their glad chorus hushed to an angry whimpering. Then they broke into cry again, and started off madly down along the brook instead of crossing it. They had a fresh fox trail; and how were they to know it was not the trail of the fox which had taken the chicken?

Red Fox, sitting solitary on his knoll, heard the noise of the chase swerve suddenly and come clamouring in his direction. At first this did not disturb him. Then all at once that subtle telepathic sense which certain individuals among the wild kindreds seem to possess signalled to him that the dogs were on a new trail. It was *his* trail they were on. *He* was the hunted one, after all. And doom was scarcely a hundred yards away. He fairly bounced into the air at the shock of this realization. Then he ran, lengthened straight out and belly to the ground, a vivid ruddy streak darting smoothly through the bushes.

It was not in the direction of home that Red Fox ran, but straight away from it. For a while the terror of the experience made his heart thump so furiously that he kept losing his breath, and was compelled to slow up from time to time. In spite of his bursts of great speed, therefore, he was unable to shake off these loud-mouthed pursuers. The suddenness and unexpectedness of it all were like a hideous dream; and added to his panic fear was a sense of injury, for he had done nothing to invite this calamity. When he reached the brook – which was shallow at this season and split up into pools and devious channels – his sheer fright led him to forget his keen aversion to a wetting, and he darted straight into it. In midstream, however, as he paused on a gravelly shoal, inherited lore and his own craft came to his aid just in time. Instead of seeking the other shore, he turned and kept on straight up mid-channel, leaping from wet rock to rock, and carefully avoiding every spot which might hold his scent. The stream was full of windings, and when the dogs reached its banks the fugitive was out of sight. His trail, too, had vanished completely from the face of the earth. Round and round in ever widening circles ran the dogs, taking in both sides of the stream, questing for the lost scent; till at last they gave up, baffled and disgusted.

Red Fox continued up the stream bed for fully a mile, long after he had satisfied himself that pursuit was at an end. Then he made a long detour to the rocky crest of the ridge, rested awhile under a bush, and descended through the early moonlight to the home den in the bank. Here he found his scatter-brained brother highly elated, having escaped the dogs without difficulty and brought home his toothsome prize in triumph. But his mother he found so anxious and apprehensive that she would not enter the burrow at all, choosing rather to take her nap in the open, under a juniper-bush, before setting out for the night's hunting. Here Red Fox curled up beside her, while the other two youngsters, ignorantly reckless, stuck to the old home nest.

That night Red Fox contented himself with catching mice in the little wild meadow up the slope. When he returned home, on the grey-pink edge of dawn, his mother and sister were already back, and sleeping just outside the door of the den, under the sheltering bush. But the triumphant young chicken-hunter was still absent. Presently there floated up on the still, fragrant air that baleful music of dogs' voices, faint and far off but unmistakable in its significance. The yellow half-breed and the black and white mongrel were again upon the trail. But what trail? That was the question that agitated the little family as they all sat upon their brushes, and cocked their ears, and listened.

With astonishing rapidity the noise grew louder and louder, coming straight towards the den. To the wise old mother there was no room to mistake the situation. Her rash and headstrong whelp had once more got the dogs upon his trail and was leading them to his home refuge. Angry and alarmed, she jumped to her feet, darted into the burrow and out again, and raced several times round and round the entrance; and first Red Fox, and then his less quick-witted sister followed her in these tactics, which they dimly began to comprehend. Then all three darted away up the hillside, and came out upon a well-known bushy ledge from which they could look back upon their home.

They had been watching but a minute or two when they saw the foolish fugitive run panting up the bank and dive into the burrow. At his very heels were the baying and barking dogs, who now set up a very different sort of chorus, a clamour of mingled impatience and delight at having run their quarry at last to earth. The black and white mongrel at once began digging furiously at the entrance, hoping to force his way in and end the whole matter without delay. But the half-breed hound preferred to wait for the men who would, he knew, soon follow and smoke the prisoner out. He contented himself with sitting back on his haunches before the door, watching his comrade's futile toil, and every now and then lifting his voice to signal the hunters to the spot. Meanwhile, the wise old mother fox on the ledge above knew as well as he what would presently happen. Having no mind to wait for the inevitable conclusion of the tragedy, she slunk away dejectedly and led the two surviving members of her litter over the ridge, across the next broad valley, and far up the slope of lonely and rugged Ringwaak, where they might have time to mature in strength and cunning before pitting their power against men.

4 *Alone in the World*

FOR some days after this sudden flight into exile, the diminished family wandered wide, having no fixed lair and feeling very much adrift. In a curious outburst of bravado or revenge, or perhaps because she for the moment grew intolerant of her long self-restraint, the mother fox one violet sunset led her two young ones in a fierce raid upon the barnyard of one of the remoter farms. It seemed a reckless piece of audacity but the old fox knew there were no dogs at this farm save a single small and useless cur; and she knew, also, that the farmer was not adept with the gun.

All was peace about the little farmyard. The golden lilac light made wonderful the chip-strewn yard and the rough, weather-beaten roofs of cabin and barn and shed. The ducks were quacking and bobbing in the wet mud about the water-trough, where some grain had been spilled. The sleepy chickens were gathering in the open front of the shed, craning their necks with little murmurings of content, and one by one hopping up to their roosts among the rafters. From the sloping pasture above the farmyard came a clatter of bars let down, and a soft tunk-a-tonk of cowbells as the cows were turned out from milking.

Into this scene of secure peace broke the three foxes, rushing silently from behind the stable. Before the busy ducks could take alarm or the sleepy chickens fly up out of danger, the enemy was among them, darting hither and thither and snapping at slim, feathered necks. Instantly arose a wild outcry of squawking, quacking, and cackling; then shrill barking from the cur, who was in the pasture with the cows, and angry shouting from the farmer, who came running at top speed down the pasture lane. The marauders cared not a jot for the barking cur, but they had no mind to await the arrival of the outraged farmer. Having settled some grudges by snapping the necks of nearly a dozen ducks and fowls, each slung a plump victim across his back and trotted leisurely away across the brown furrows of the potato-field towards the woods. Just as they were about to disappear under the branches they all three turned and glanced back at the farmer, where he stood by the water-trough shaking his fists at them in impotent and childish rage.

This audacious exploit seemed in some way to break up the little family. In some way, at this time, the two youngsters seemed to realize their capacity for complete independence and self-reliance; and at the same moment, as it were, the mother in some subtle fashion let slip the reins of her influence. All three became indifferent to each other; and without any misunderstanding or ill will each went his or her own way. As for Red Fox, with a certain bold confidence in his own craft, he turned his face back towards the old bank on the hillside, the old den behind the juniper-bush, and the little mouse-haunted meadow by the friendly brook.

As he neared the old home, with the memory of tragic events strong upon him, Red Fox went very

circumspectly, as if he thought the dogs might still be frequenting the place. But he found it, of course, a bright solitude. The dry slope lay warm in the sun, the scattered juniper-bushes stood prickly and dark as of old, and unseen behind its screen of leafage the brook near by babbled pleasantly as of old over its little falls and shoals. But where had been the round, dark door of his home was now a gaping gash of raw, red earth. The den had been dug out to its very bottom. Being something of a philosopher in his young way, and quite untroubled by sentiment, Red Fox resumed possession of the bank. For the present he made his lair under the bush on top of the bank, where his father had been wont to sleep. He knew the bank was a good place for a fox to inhabit, being warm, dry, secluded, and easy to dig. Well under the shelter of another juniper, at the extreme lower end of the bank and quite out of sight of the old den, he started another burrow to serve him for winter quarters.

Engrossed in the pursuit of experience and provender, Red Fox had no time for loneliness. Every hour of the day or night that he could spare from sleep was full of interest for him. The summer had been a benignant one, favourable to all the wild kindreds, and now the red and saffron autumn woods were swarming with furtive life. With a flicker of white fluffy tails, like diminutive powder-puffs, the brown rabbits were bounding through the underbrush on all sides. The dainty wood-mice, delicate-footed as shadows, darted and squeaked among the brown tree roots, while in every grassy glade or patch of browning meadow the field-mice and the savage little shrews went scurrying in throngs. The whirring coveys of the partridge went volleying down the aisles of golden birch, their strong brown wings making a cheerful but sometimes startling noise; and the sombre tops of the fir groves along the edge of the lower fields were loud with crows. In this populous world Red Fox found hunting so easy that he had time for more investigating and gathering of experience.

At this time his curiosity was particularly excited by men and their ways; and he spent a great deal of his time around the skirts of the farmsteads, watching and considering. But certain precautions his sagacious young brain never forgot. No trail of his led between the valley fields and his burrow on the hillside. Before descending towards the lowlands he would always climb the hill, cross a spur of the ridge, and traverse a wide, stony gulch where his trail was quickly and irretrievably lost. Descending from the other side of this gulch, his track seemed always as if it came over from the other valley, below Ringwaak. Moreover, when he reached the farms he resolutely ignored ducks, turkeys, chickens – and, indeed, in the extremity of his wisdom, the very rats and mice which frequented yard and rick. How was he to know that the rats which enjoyed the hospitality of man's fodder stack were less dear to him than the chickens who sheltered in his shed? He had no intention of drawing down upon his inexperienced head the vengeance of a being whose powers he had not yet learned to define. Nevertheless, when he found beneath a tree at the back of an orchard a lot of plump, worm-bitten plums, he had no hesitation in feasting upon the juicy sweets; for the idea that man might be interested in any such inanimate objects had not yet penetrated his wits.

Another precaution which this young investigator of man and manners very carefully observed was to keep aloof from the farm of the yellow half-breed hound. That was the chief point of danger. The big black and white mongrel, whose scent was not keen, he did not so very much dread. But when he saw the two dogs playing together, then he knew that the most likely thing in the world was a hunting expedition of some kind; and he would make all haste to seek a less precarious neighbourhood. Towards dogs in general he had no very pronounced aversion, such as his cousin the wolf entertained; but these two dogs in particular he feared and hated. Whenever, gazing down from one of his numerous lookouts or watch-towers, he saw the two excitedly mussing over one of his old, stale trails – which straggled all about the valley – his thin, dark muzzle would wrinkle in vindictive scorn. In his tenacious memory a grudge was growing which might some day, if occasion offered, exact sharp payment.

Among the animals associated in the young fox's mind with man there was only one of which he stood in awe. As he was stealing along one day in the shadow of a garden fence, he heard just above him a sharp, malevolent, spitting sound, verging instantly into a most vindictive growl. Very much startled, he jumped backward and looked up. There on top of the fence crouched a small, greyish, dark striped animal, with a round face, round, greenish, glaring eyes, long tail fluffed out, and high-arched back. At the sound of that bitter voice, the glare of those furious eyes, Red Fox's memory went back to the dreadful day when the lynx had pounced at him from the thicket. This spitting, threatening creature on the fence was, of course, nothing like the lynx in size; and Red Fox felt sure that he was much more than a match for it in fair fight. He had no wish to try conclusions with it, however. For some seconds he stood eyeing it nervously. Then the cat, divining his apprehensions, advanced slowly along the top of the fence, spitting explosively and uttering the most malignant yowls. Red Fox stood his ground till the hideous apparition was within five or six feet of him. Then he turned and fled ignominiously; and the cat, the instant he was gone, scurried wildly for the house as if a pack of fiends were after her.

Among the man creatures whom Red Fox amused himself by watching at this period, there were two who made a peculiar impression upon him, two whom he particularly differentiated from all the rest. One of these was the farmer–hunter, Jabe Smith, who owned the black and white mongrel – he whose stray shot had caused the death of Red Fox's father. This fact, of course, Red Fox did not know – nor, indeed, one must confess, would he have greatly considered it had he known. Nevertheless, in some subtle way the young fox came to apprehend that this Jabe Smith was among all the man creatures of the settlement, particularly dangerous and implacable – a man to be assiduously studied in order to be assiduously avoided. It was from Jabe Smith that the furry young investigator got his first idea of a gun. He saw the man come out of the house with a long black stick in his hands, and point it at a flock of ducks just winging overhead. He saw red flame and blue-white smoke belch from the end of the black stick. He heard an appalling burst of thunder which flapped and roared among the hills. And he saw one of the ducks turn over in its flight and plunge headlong down to earth. Yes, of a certainty this man was very dangerous. And when, a few evenings later, as the colour was fading out of the chill autumn sky, he saw the man light a fire of chips down in the farmyard, to boil potatoes for the pigs, his dread and wonder grew tenfold. These red and yellow tongues that leaped so venomously around the black pot – terrible creatures called forth out of the chips at the touch of the man's hand – were manifestly akin to the red thing which had jumped from the end of the stick and killed the voyaging duck. Even when away over in the other valley, hunting, or when curled up safely under his juniper-bush on the bank, Red Fox was troubled with apprehensions about the man of the fire. He never felt himself quite secure except when he had the evidence of his own eyes as to what the mysterious being was up to.

The one other human creature whom Red Fox honoured with his interest was the Boy. The Boy lived on one of the farther farms, one of the largest and most prosperous, one equipped with all that a backwoods farm should have except, as it chanced, a dog. The Boy had once had a dog, a wise bull terrier to which he was so much attached that when it died its place was kept sacredly vacant. He was a sturdy, gravely cheerful lad, the Boy, living much by himself, playing by himself, devoted to swimming, canoeing, skating, riding, and all such strenuous outdoor work of the muscles, yet studious, no less of books than of the fascinating wilderness life about him. But of all his occupations woodcraft was that which most engrossed his interest. In the woods he moved as noiselessly as the wild kindreds themselves, saw as keenly, heard as alertly, as they.

And because he was quiet, and did not care to kill, and because his boyish blue eyes were steady, many of the wild kindreds came to regard him with a curious lack of aversion. It was not that the most amiable of them cared a rap for him, or for any human being; but ceasing to greatly fear him, they became indifferent. He was able, therefore, to observe many interesting details of life in that silent, populous, secretive wilderness which to humanity in general seems a solitude.

To Red Fox the Boy became an object of interest only second to Jabe Smith. But in this case fear and antagonism were almost absent. He watched the Boy from sheer curiosity, almost as the Boy might have watched him if given the same sort of chance. It puzzled Red Fox to see the Boy go so soundlessly through the woods, watching, listening, expectant, like one of the wild folk. And in an effort to solve the puzzle he was given to following warily in the Boy's trail – but so warily that his presence was never guessed.

For weeks Red Fox kept studying the Boy in this way, whenever he had a chance; but it was some time before the Boy got a chance to study Red Fox. Then it came about in a strange fashion. One afternoon, some time after Red Fox had discovered and enjoyed the fallen plums in the orchard, he came upon a wild grape-vine on the edge of the valley, loaded with ripe fruit. Grape-vines were a rare growth in the Ringwaak region; but this one, growing in a sheltered and fertile nook, was a luxuriant specimen of its kind. It had draped itself in serpentine tangles over a couple of dying trees; and the clusters of its fruit were of a most alluring purple.

Red Fox looked on this unknown fruit and felt sure

that it was good. He remembered the plums, and his lips watered. One small bunch, swinging low down on a vagrant shoot of vine, he sampled. It was all that he had fancied it might be. But the rest of the bursting, purple clusters hung out of reach. Leap as he might, straight up in the air, with tense muscles and eagerly snapping jaws, he could reach not a single grape. Around and around the masses of vine he circled, looking for a point of attack. Then he attempted climbing, but in vain. His efforts in this direction were as futile as his jumping and the grapes remained inviolate.

Red Fox was resourceful and persistent; but there are occasions when resourcefulness and persistence prove a snare. He sat down on his haunches and carefully thought out the situation. At one place he had found that, owing to the twists of the great vine around its supporting tree, he could scale the trunk for a distance of five or six feet. This seemed useless, however, as there were no grapes within reach at that point; but he observed at length a spot that he might jump to after climbing as high as he could – a spot where a tangle of vines might afford him foothold, and where the luscious bunches would hang all about his head. He lost no more time in considering, but climbed, poised himself carefully, gathered his muscles, and sprang out into the air.

The feat was well calculated and exactly accomplished, and Red Fox alighted safely among the grapes. But what he had not allowed for, or even guessed at, was the yielding elasticity of the vines. They gave way in all directions, quite eccentrically and inconsistently. For several seconds he made a frantic struggle to keep up, clutching with paws and jaws. Then, squirming and baffled, he fell through.

Unhappily for him, however, he did not fall through completely. The tangle of stems that would not sustain him seemed equally resolved not to let him go. An obstinate twist of vine hooked itself about one hind leg, above the joint, and held him fast, swinging head downward.

The luckless adventurer writhed up against himself, striving to loose that relentless clutch with his teeth. But the facile yielding of the vines gave him no purchase, and every struggle he made but drew the snare tighter. When he realized his predicament, he became panic-stricken, and fell to a violent kicking and struggling and swinging which made loud disturbance in the leafage. This he kept up for several minutes, till at last, utterly exhausted, he hung motionless, swaying in the brown-green shadow, his tongue out piteously and his eyes half-shut.

Just at this moment, by chance, arrived the Boy. His quick ear had caught from a distance the unwonted thrashing of leafage at a time when all the air was still. Drawing near very stealthily, in order to miss nothing of what there might be to be seen, he came up just as the captive seemed to be dying. One fresh struggle of fright convulsed the young fox's limbs; then, realizing that the situation was hopeless, he relaxed to apparent lifelessness, his eyes closed to a narrow, deathlike slit.

The Boy, with instant commiseration, sprang forward and loosed the coil, grieving that he had not come in time to save the handsome creature's life. He had a rather special interest in foxes, admiring their cleverness and self-possession. Now, his grey eyes full of pity, he held up the limp form in his arms, smoothing the brilliant, vivid, luxuriant fur. He had never before had a chance to examine a fox so rich in colour. Finally, deciding that he could now have a splendid foxskin without any qualms of conscience, he turned his face homeward, flinging the body carelessly over his shoulder by the hind legs.

At this moment, however, just as he was leaving, there flashed across his mind's eye a vision of the great purple grape-clusters, which he had seen when quite too much preoccupied to notice them. Could he leave those ripe grapes behind him? No, indeed! He turned back again eagerly, flung the dead fox down, and fell to feasting till mouth and fingers were purple. His appetite satisfied, satiated indeed, he then filled his hat, and at last, with a sigh of contentment, faced about to pick up the dead fox. For a moment he stared in amazement, and rubbed his eyes. The fox he had flung down so carelessly was the deadest looking fox he had ever seen. But now, there was no fox there. Then, swiftly, because he understood the wild creatures, it flashed upon him how cunningly he had been fooled. With a quiet little chuckle of appreciation he went home, bearing no trophy but his hatful of wild grapes.

5 *Mating and Mastery*

IMMEASURABLY elated by his success in outwitting the Boy, Red Fox now ran some risk of growing overbold and underrating the superiority of man. Fortunately for himself, however, he presently received a sharp lesson. He was stealthily trailing Jabe Smith, one crisp morning, when the latter was out with his gun, looking for partridges. A whirr of unseen wings chancing to make Jabe turn sharply in his tracks, he caught sight of a bright red fox shrinking back into the underbrush. Jabe was a quick shot. He up with his gun and fired instantly. His charge, however, was only in for partridges, and the shot was a long one. A few of the small leaden pellets struck Red Fox in the flank. They penetrated no deeper than the skin; but the shock was daunting, and they stung most viciously. In his amazement and fright he sprang straight into the air. Then, straightening himself out, belly to earth, he fled off in a red streak among the trunks of the young white birches. For days he was tormented with a smarting and itching in his side, which nothing could allay; and for weeks he kept well away from the haunts of men.

About this time the young fox met with several surprises. One morning, emerging from under his juniper-bush in the first pale rose of dawn, he found a curious, thin, sparkling incrustation on the dead leaves, and the brown grasses felt stiff and brittle under his tread. Much puzzled, he sniffed at the hoar-frost, and tasted it, and found it had nothing to give tongue or nose but a sensation of cold. The air, too, had grown unwontedly cold, so that his thoughts reverted to the burrow which he had been digging. Both the cold and the sparkling hoarfrost fled away as the sun got high; but Red Fox set himself at once to work completing his burrow. Thereafter he occupied it, and forgot all about the lair beneath the juniper-bush.

Shortly after this he made his first acquaintance with the miracle of the ice. One chilly morning in the half-light, when the upper sky was just taking on the first rose-stains of dawn, he stopped to drink at a little pool. To his amazement, his muzzle came in contact with some hard but invisible substance, intervening between his nose and the water. At first he backed off in wary suspicion, and glanced all about him to see if anything else had gone wrong in the world. Then he sniffed at the ice, and lapped it tentatively and finally, growing bolder, thrust at it so hard with his nose that it broke. This seemed to solve the mystery to his satisfaction, so he slaked his thirst and went about his hunting. Later in the day, however, happening to drink again at the same pool, he was surprised to find that the strange, hard, invisible, breakable substance had all gone. He hunted for it anxiously, and was utterly mystified until he found some remnants still unthawed; whereupon he was once more content, seeming to think the phenomenon quite adequately explained.

This surprise over hoarfrost and ice, however, was

nothing to his troubled astonishment on the coming of the first snow. One morning, after a hard hunting expedition which had occupied the first half of the night, he slept till after daylight. During his sleep the snow had come, covering the ground to the depth of about an inch. When he poked his nose out from the burrow, the flurry was about over, but here and there a light, belated flake still loitered down.

At his first sight of a world from which all colour had been suddenly wiped out, Red Fox started back – shrank back, indeed, to the very bottom of his den. The universal and inexplicable whiteness appalled him. In a moment or two, however, curiosity restored his courage, and he returned to the door. But he would not venture forth. Cautiously thrusting his head out, he stared in every direction. What was this white stuff covering everything but the naked hardwood branches? It looked to him like feathers. If so, there must have been great hunting. But no, his nose soon informed him it was not feathers. Presently he took up a little in his mouth, and was puzzled to find that it vanished almost instantly. At last he stepped out, to investigate the more fully. But, to his disgust, he found that he got his feet wet, as well as cold. He hated getting his feet wet, so he slipped back at once into the den and licked them dry.

For an hour or more Red Fox sulked and marvelled in his dry retreat. Then as the air grew soft the snow dissolved away in patches, and he came out, stepping fastidiously. But all through the morning he was too much interested to do any hunting. Not till late afternoon did hunger make him forget this inexplicable thing that had so changed the face of his world, and drive him forth to the serious business of life. When, however, some ten days later, on the heels of an iron frost, the snow came in earnest, he had completely adapted himself to it and treated storm and cold alike with supreme unconcern.

In all this time Red Fox had had not a glimpse of his mother or sister, though their trails he had crossed from time to time, recognizing them unerringly by the scent. At these reminiscent trails he always sniffed with a kind of pleasure, yet he felt no impulse to follow them up and renew old intimacies. Other foxes, strangers, he caught sight of in the distance once in a while; but his impulse, like that of his kind, was to avoid companionship, which is apt to mean complication. Moreover, he had no wish to encourage trespassers upon what he now regarded as his own peculiar range. Young as he was, he was nevertheless so vigorous and well grown as to pass readily for a fine yearling; and he was quite prepared to fight in defence of his preemptions.

This freedom from interference could hardly be expected to last, however, without some price's being exacted. Red Fox had a possession which many of the wild creatures coveted – to wit, a burrow that was secret, dry, and warm. In his absences it had been explored by various stealthy wanderers – weasel, woodchuck, mink, and black snake – but they had all taken care to be well out of it before the owner's return. One surly old woodchuck, a battle-scarred veteran of a courage to match his ill-temper, went so far as to establish himself in the door of the burrow with the purpose of fighting for its possession. But Red Fox happened to be away on a long chase in the other valley; and, after the old woodchuck had waited for a couple of hours in vain, his valour waned. He remembered that there were other burrows, if not to be stolen then to be dug; and he remembered, too, that the issues of war are doubtful. He wandered down to the nearest turnip-field, was caught in his pillaging by the black and white mongrel, and killed after a magnificent fight. And Red Fox never guessed what a stern struggle had been spared him. Strong and clever as he was, he doubtless would have won; but he would have carried scars thereafter.

One day when Red Fox came trotting contentedly home with a partridge in his jaws, he found the fresh tracks of another fox leading ahead of him straight to the den. Sniffing at these, he realized that the visitor was a stranger; and instantly a vague antagonism lifted the hair along his back. To him any visit was intrusion at least, if not invasion. He hurried up to the juniper-bush – and was met by the sight of the intruder standing half-way out of the entrance to the den, with ears back, teeth bare, impudent defiance in the gleam of his narrowed eyes.

The heart of Red Fox swelled with a hitherto unknown passion, a mingling of injury and savage rage. Dropping the partridge, he sprang silently upon the intruder, who met him willingly enough just below the juniper-bush. There was no sparring for position, but both grappled on the instant, each with a snap and a grip; and, locked in a red furry ball, they rolled about three yards down the bank. Here they brought up sharply against a stone, Red Fox on top, and worrying fiercely at the side of his enemy's neck.

Jammed down against the stone, the trespasser was

now getting much the worst of the battle. Blood, his own and his adversary's, flowed into his eyes, half-blinding him. Suddenly he decided that he had been in the wrong – and he made a swift repentance. With a vehement heave and wriggle he doubled himself up, emerged between Red Fox's hind legs, and sprang away. Red Fox wheeled, eyed him for a second, then rushed for him again. The stranger did not pause to apologize or explain, but bounded right over the nearest bush and made off through the underbrush at a pace which showed his sincerity. Red Fox followed for perhaps a hundred yards, and then, greatly elated by his triumph, returned to the den to lick his hurts.

It was less than a week after this encounter when another strange fox appeared. Red Fox was just setting out for his afternoon hunt, when he saw the stranger halting irresolutely at the edge of a thicket some twenty yards below the den. His hair bristled up at once, and he advanced, stepping delicately on his toes, savagely inhospitable and ripe for another fight. But there seemed to be no hostility in the stranger's attitude.

It was irresolution, rather, and an impulse to flight. So it came about that, as Red Fox advanced, his enmity began to cool, till his motive in drawing near was little more than a desire to find out what the visitor wanted. The angry ridge of hair along his neck and shoulders sank down, the dangerous gleam faded out of his alert eyes. The stranger, waiting on tiptoe, seemed always on the point of running away; yet never did, but kept watching Red Fox's approach over her shoulder.

When he found himself within half a dozen yards of

the diffident stranger, Red Fox halted and sat up, his head cocked sideways, his jaws half-open, his tongue lightly hanging out, his face a picture of bland but eager interest. The stranger, apparently somewhat reassured, now permitted herself to sit down also, turning so as to face him. In this position they eyed each other in silence for a minute or two, mutually benevolent. Then Red Fox jumped up briskly, trotted over to the visitor, and sniffed at her cordially. Both seemed highly gratified at the encounter; and, after gamboling together for a few minutes, and chasing each other about, they went off side by side through the underbrush, seemingly bent upon a partnership in the chase.

Filled with pride and an exultation utterly new to his heart, Red Fox trotted on, with eyes fixed upon the slim companion at his side, his eyes wrinkled and mouth open in an expression of foolish content. The young she, however, kept her eyes and wits about her, keen for the hunt and apparently indifferent to her conquest. Here she pounced upon an unwary foraging mouse. Here she captured a maimed snowbird, as it was hopping in panic fear towards the covert of a juniper thicket. And at last, creeping with indescribable stealth around the roots of a huge beech-tree, she seized a drowsing rabbit which her skilful nose had discovered to her. Her skill and prowess delighted Red Fox beyond measure; and, as the twain feasted together on the stained snow, their mating was cemented with the blood of the long-eared victim.

After this capture the pair turned back homeward by a long circle which brought them close to the skirts of the settlement. Here, as luck would have it, their fresh trail was picked up by the half-breed hound as

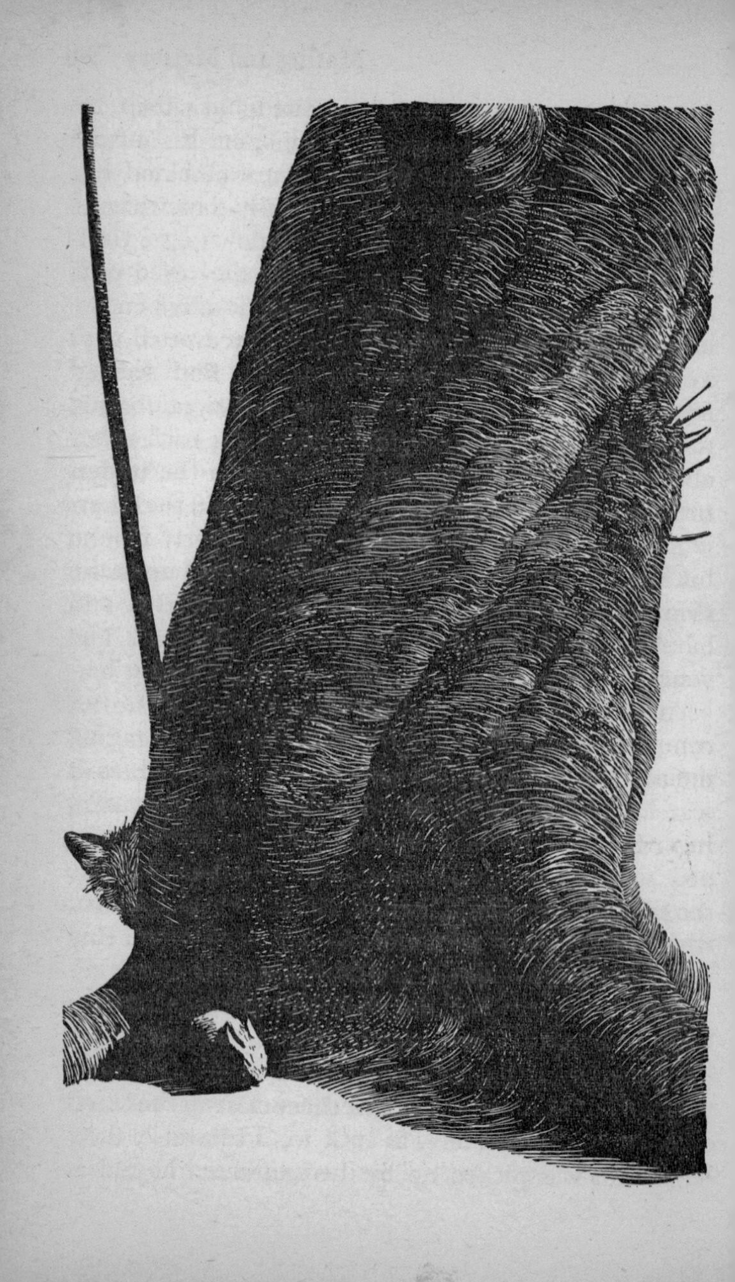

he was trotting lazily down the road to visit the farm of his comrade, the black and white mongrel. So fresh and so alluring was the scent that he could not wait for company, but broke into joyous cry and dashed into the woods alone.

Red Fox and his mate were less than half a mile from the road when that ominous sound arose on the clear, frosty air. They stopped short, stood, each with a foot uplifted, as motionless as statues, and listened critically. There was but one voice in the cry. Plainly there was but one foe in pursuit. They looked at each other searchingly, and seemed to come to an understanding without discussion. Then they resumed their journey, trotting perhaps a little faster than before, but certainly not running away. Red Fox was in no mood to run away; and his slim comrade seemed to have lost that timorousness of nature which she had displayed towards himself a few hours earlier.

As they were making no haste, the voice of the pursuing enemy drew swiftly nearer. At last it was just the other side of a line of young spruce-trees, not two score paces behind them. Red Fox's heart was thumping, but there was no thought of flight in it. He stopped and whirled about to face the peril. As he did so, the she fox turned with him, undaunted as he. Then, with a soft crashing of fir-branches, the loud enemy burst into view.

The dog had covered half the space between before he seemed to notice that the two foxes were not fleeing, but awaiting him. He was surprised, and stopped abruptly, while the high-carried feather of his tail drooped in indecision. This but for a second or two, however; for what were these two slender antagonists to him? Finding voice again, he dashed forward. And the two foxes, with a shrill, threatening bark, ran to meet him.

Now the half-breed's speciality was distinctly not fighting, but trailing; and he was taken aback by this most unexpected and irregular attitude of the two foxes. As he hesitated, he suddenly found himself in the midst of a demoralizing mix-up. Frantically he snapped his big jaws at his elusive assailants, but got only a few mouthfuls of soft fur, so nimble were they. In the meantime he was getting bitten smartly on both hind legs, and slashed on neck and dewlap till the blood ran copiously. Those assaults upon his hind legs terrified him particularly. He was afraid of getting hamstrung. This fear in a moment grew into a panic. With all his strength he shook himself free. His proud tail tucked shamelessly between his legs, he turned and fled for home. The two foxes ran after him a little way, in mere pretence of pursuit, then, extremely elated over their easy triumph, resumed their journey towards the den on the hillside.

6 *Burning Spur and Blinding Claw*

THE newcomer took to the dry, warm burrow very kindly, and proceeded at once to enlarge it beyond the immediate needs of Red Fox himself. Once fairly settled, the two adopted separate ranges, Red Fox hunting down the valley and eastward along the lower slopes, which was, of course, the more perilous tract; while his mate took the safer region to westward of the den, where there were no settlements and no dogs, and only an occasional camp of harmless lumbermen to beware of. Lynxes and bears, of course, were more numerous on her range, but these she well knew how to evade, so she troubled her head little about them. It was man, and the ways of man, and the allies and followers of man, that held her shrewd spirit in awe.

During the first part of the winter the abundance which had marked the preceding autumn continued. But soon after Christmas a succession of heavy snow-falls, followed by tremendous and unrelenting frosts, made game very scarce. Many of the weaker birds and animals died of cold or starvation. Others took refuge in their securest coverts. Some of the winter dwellers, among the birds, unwillingly drifted south to more hospitable skies; while down from the north came hungry flocks of crossbills and big, stupid, rosy-headed grosbeaks, followed by those savage and insatiable marauders, the white arctic hawk and the great white arctic owl. These dangerous intruders on the range played havoc among the rabbits and squirrels, the mice and grouse and crows, who were all unused to their mode of attack and apt to be deceived by their colour. Scarce as game was by reason of the cold, they speedily made it scarcer; and the foxes hated them virulently.

In this lean season the thoughts of Red Fox turned longingly to the protected and well-fed dependents of the dangerous men creatures. Nevertheless, he would not permit himself to visit the hen-roosts of the neighbouring valley farms. He was too sagacious to invite fate. But he remembered that over towards Ringwaak, across the ridge, on the range of a rival fox, there were other hen-roosts and duck-pens. And one night, when there was a late-setting moon, he started over the ridge, while his mate set out for a rabbit hunt among the fir thickets to the north-west of the buried and silent brook.

On a certain farm, sleeping in the blue-white, frosty moonlight, Red Fox found the little door of the chicken-house left open in spite of the bitter cold. There was no dog on that farm. The low-roofed, roomy cabin was silent, and no light gleamed from its windows. The barn was quiet, save for the hushed munching of the cows in their stanchions, the occasional stamping of the restless horses in their stalls. A big grey cat, footing in leisurely fashion across the snowy yard, caught sight of the prowling, brush-tailed visitor, and with a frightened *pfiff* scuttled up to the roof of the wood-shed, yowling angrily. Red Fox eyed her for a second, decided that she was a negligible factor in his problem, and poked his sharp nose cautiously into the little door of the chicken-house. The smell within of warm, fat, well-fed, comfortable hens was most alluring. He yielded to the delicate temptation, and slipped in.

The moonlight streamed, a wide, white flood, through a spacious window just opposite the roosts. Red Fox saw at once that the farmer had arranged the roosts with the utmost consideration for a fox's lack of skill in climbing. The hens were fat and heavy – mostly of mixed Brahma, Cochin, and Plymouth Rock descent – so their owner had placed a long, sloping plank, with cleats across it, to enable them to hop up to their perches without the effort of flight. Moreover, the perches themselves were arranged about a foot and a half above a broad shelf, which served to protect the nests underneath. It was altogether a most up-to-date arrangement, in the approved design of the poultry books. But if Red Fox had had the designing of it himself, he could not have made it to meet his own requirements more perfectly.

Pausing just inside the door, in a patch of black shadow, he carefully and calculatingly surveyed the perches. The hens were all asleep, but the cock, a wary sleeper, was awake. He had heard no noise from Red Fox's furtive entrance, but some subtle perception of danger had wakened him. His keen, bold eyes detected something unusual in that patch of shadow. Stretching out his neck and fine, snaky head, he uttered a long-drawn *quee-ee-ee-ee* of warning interrogation.

Red Fox paid no attention to this soft, unterrifying sound. Having made up his mind, he darted fearlessly up the sloping plank, ran along the raised platform, and seized the fourth hen from the end, a fat, alluring, thick-feathered Brahma. One quick crunch of his jaws on the victim's neck, and the fluttering mass of feathers made no more struggle. Red Fox jerked the prize across his shoulders, turned, and trotted quite deliberately down the plank. When he was about half-way down, however, a most astonishing thing happened. He was all at once enveloped, as it seemed, in a cloud of buffeting wings, something sharp and apparently burning hot drove deep into the side of his neck, and a heavy, soft body struck him so vehemently that he rolled completely over and fell heavily to the floor, while the limp, sprawling mass of his victim tumbled over his face, blinding and confusing him.

The cock, who had been watching with such alert suspicion, was not of the same breed as the hens. He was no awkward Cochin or Brahma, but a long-spurred, hard-feathered, clean-headed, thoroughbred, black-red Game. This was Red Fox's misfortune.

As Red Fox picked himself up, bewildered, the cock flew again, buffeting his head again with strong, swift wings, and again striking one of those dagger-like spurs into his neck. The wound caused a burning anguish; and this time it was dangerously near the root of the ear, which gave Red Fox a qualm of apprehension. What if that elusive weapon should find his eyes? Filled with rage, he made a savage rush at his trim assailant. But the cock was ready, cool and sagacious. Springing lightly into the air, he evaded the animal's rush, sailed clean over his head, and in passing delivered another of those daunting spur strokes. The point went deep into the upper part of the enemy's snout, about an inch below the eye. The pain was intense; but the terror of those strokes counted for more than the pain with Red Fox. He could take punishment with unsurpassable pluck, but the risk of losing his eyes filled him with panic. He wanted no more to do with this strange and terrible antagonist. With head low down, to shun a repetition of the stroke, he darted out through the little door. As he went, those dread wings beat again upon his back, and both spurs sank into his rump. Thoroughly cowed, he fled in ignominy across the field and into the woods; and the shrill crowing of the victor taunted him, echoing at his heels across the radiant snow.

Into the deep shadows he fled, over the snow-hidden brook, across the little, shining glades, through the dense fir thickets, the tangled, leafless underbrush, the huge, silent groves of ancient trees, and never paused till he came in view of the familiar bank on the hillside and the juniper-bush, behind which lay the door of his den. Here he halted for a second. But as he did so he saw on the top of the bank above the den a sight which drove all the panic terror out of his heart. Forgetting his pain and his bleeding wounds, he uttered a shrill yelp of fury and dashed forward again at a pace which no terror had had power to teach his feet.

While Red Fox was suffering his castigation at the wings and spurs of the heroic game-cock, his mate was trotting homeward from a fairly successful hunt among the boulders of the upper ridge. As she came noiselessly along the top of the bank, her back to the glare of moonlight, she caught sight of a weasel approaching, some distance away among the tree-trunks. Perceiving from his manner that she had not been detected, she slipped behind the screen of a thin bush, crouched, and waited for the weasel to come to his doom. Nearer, nearer he came; and tenser, tenser grew the attitude of the ambushed hunter as she held herself gathered for the final spring and rush.

It chanced that in the meantime one of those great, silent, white marauders from the north was winnowing soundlessly through the spaces of the woods, his round, bright eyes, hard like glass, glaring into every bush and covert. He was fiercely hungry. The weasel, approaching through the broken shadows, he did not see; but the fox, crouching behind the little bush, he could not help seeing. The direction of his wide, downy-feathered wings changed instantly, and he swept up behind the unsuspecting fox like a drifting wraith of white vapour. The weasel just then seemed near enough to be rushed; so the fox sprang right through the bush. Even while she was in mid-air, the owl swooped, and struck, his terrible talons sinking deep into her loins and back. With a mighty beating of wings and yelpings of amazement and pain, the two came down together on the snow.

Many a time before had the great white owl hunted foxes, and conquered them, and devoured them; but they had been the little arctic foxes, less strong, less cunning, and less indomitable than their ruddy southern kin. Now he found that he had entered upon a difficult adventure. In spite of the cruel pain inflicted by those gripping talons, the dauntless little vixen writhed backward and upward, and bit swiftly with snapping, slashing jaws. Three times she tried for a hold, undaunted by the beating of the great wings which strove, but not quite successfully, to lift her from the snow. Three times she got only a mouthful of downy, clinging, choking feathers. Then, her quick sagacity coming to her aid as she felt herself being lifted, she reached farther up and caught the base of the enemy's wing. With all the strength of desperation, she ground her jaws together, and presently the strong bones went with a crunch. Instantly she felt herself solid on the snow again. The lifting strain ceased. The great wing trailed nervelessly.

Crippled though he was, the robber from the north was game. It was no longer hunting, but fighting, that he found himself engaged in, and at an unwonted, utterly unexpected disadvantage. He now brought his powerful beak into play, and tore furiously at his adversary's flank. But the fox, active and crafty, kept her hold on the broken wing, and strove to force the owl over on his back. The latter had to loose the grip of his talons and flap frantically with his one effective wing to avert this fatal catastrophe. At the same time, however, his knife-edged, powerful beak, hooked like a sickle for the rending of tough hides, was doing bloody work on the slim vixen's back and sides. It was just at this point – while the issue of the battle yet hung in doubt, and it would have taken a wise onlooker to say which had the advantage – that Red Fox burst upon the scene.

It was with a fighting rage, intensified by shame at his recent defeat as well as by devotion to his mate, that he came into the fray. In utter silence he darted up the bank, and sprang. The great bird saw, and met him with a blinding blow of his wing; but Red Fox in the next instant bore him backward, clawing wildly and vainly flapping. That formidable beak tore once and again into Red Fox's flesh. Then the latter's teeth found the enemy's throat; and in one heart-beat the fight came to an end. The great bird lay motionless, sprawled upon his back on the blood-stained snow.

The two foxes touched noses sympathetically, then fell to licking each other's wounds. This took a good half-hour of that enduring patience in which the wilderness kindred are so marvellously endowed. The glass-clear moonlight bathed the two intimate figures as they stood there painstakingly caressing on the open crest of the bank. From a safe refuge near by, the weasel watched them for a long time in wonder, hating them, but rejoicing at the death of the great owl, who was to him a far more dangerous enemy than any fox. At length, the wounds seeming to be all adequately doctored, Red Fox slipped down the slope and into the den, scrupulously ignoring the body of the owl. This was his mate's prey, and he would not seem to claim any rights in it. As for her, she understood her rights perfectly. The great, loose, floppy agglomeration of feathers was too much for her to carry in the usual fox fashion, so she briskly dragged it down the slope to the mouth of the den. Pulling one wing inside, that no passing forest thief might be tempted to try and make off with it, she lay down just within and rested with her fore paws upon the prize, waiting till they both should feel sufficiently rested to make their breakfast upon it. A wandering mink slipped by, and paused to look in hostile wonder at the great white marauder of the north, terrible even in death. But he knew that sharp eyes watched him from within the den, and he had no mind for closer investigation. He darted away snakily towards the brook, where he had certain hidden runways beneath the edges of the ice. And the bright emptiness of the cold settled down once more upon the forest.

7 *The Foiling of the Traps*

ONE night soon after these painful episodes, while the moonlight was yet bright on the glittering wilderness, the two foxes were playing together in the shining lane which the snow-covered channel of the brook made through the forest. Their wounds had given little trouble to theiry hardy and healthy flesh. Their hunting had been good in the early part of the night. They were young, extremely well satisfied with themselves and with each other; and the only occupation that met their mood was to chase each other round and round in short circles, leaping over each other's backs, and occasionally grappling, rising on their hind legs, and biting at each other's throats with every pretence of ferocity. Unlike dogs, they made no noise in their play, except for the hushed rustle and patter of scurrying and pushing feet, the occasional swish and crackle of the bushes they disturbed.

Suddenly, as they met after a circling rush, they checked themselves as they were just about to grapple, and stood motionless, staring at a strange trail. It was the track of a man on snow-shoes. Their noses, anxiously inquiring, presently assured them that the trail was many hours old. Then they subjected it to the most wondering and searching examination. Surely there could be no creature with such stupendous feet as that inhabiting their wilderness. But, if there were, it behoved them to find out all about it, the more securely to avoid encountering such a monster.

About these great tracks, and especially near the centre of each, where the depression was deepest, there clung the strong man scent, which puzzled them the more as they knew that the feet of man made no such prints. Then Red Fox identified the scent still more exactly, recognizing it as that of his especial antipathy, the dreaded dispenser of fire and noise and death, Jabe Smith. Upon this he came to realize that the gigantic tracks were made by something attached to Jabe Smith's feet. For what purpose, or to what use, the man should so enlarge his feet Red Fox could not conceive; but he knew that men were always mysterious, and he was content to let the question go at that. The point that interested both the foxes now was, Whither did the tracks lead? What was the man's business here in their woods?

All thought of play laid aside, they now took up the trail, following cautiously, with every sense on the alert. The trail led towards the farthest and wildest section of the she fox's range. At length it came to a halt, where it crossed a well-marked runway of her own. The snow was trampled and disturbed at this point, and just here, where the runway was narrowed by a thick bush on either side, lay the frozen head and neck of a chicken. Red Fox, for all his natural wariness, was starting forward to investigate this prize; but his mate, who had somehow obtained a certain knowledge of traps, thrust him aside so brusquely that he realized the presence of an unknown peril. Then, and not till then, he noticed that at that point, around and beneath the chicken head, there were no fox tracks visible. They had evidently been covered with snow. While he was considering this ominous fact, his mate moved forward with the extreme of caution, sniffing at the snow before every step. With intense interest he watched her, realizing that she knew something of which he, for all his craft, was ignorant. In a moment or two she stopped, and began sniffing around the point at which she had stopped. The care she displayed in this amounted to timidity, and convinced Red Fox that something terribly dangerous lay hidden beneath the snow. In a moment or two the prudent investigator began to dig, pawing away the snow with light, delicate, surface strokes; and presently she revealed a small, dark, menacing thing, made of the same hard, cold substance which Red Fox had observed that so many of man's implements were made of. The snow on the middle of the trap the wise little she dared not disturb; and she flatly discouraged any very close examination on Red Fox's part. But she gave him to understand that this was one of the cunningest and most deadly of all the devices which that incomprehensible creature, man, was wont to employ against the wild kindreds. And she also made him understand that unexpectant blessings, like the chicken head, or other unusual dainties, when found scattered with seeming generosity about the forest ways, were pretty sure to indicate at least one trap in the immediate neighbourhood. Leaving the treacherous thing unmasked, so that no other of the forest dwellers might be betrayed by it, the two foxes resumed the trapper's trail, to find out what more treasons he had plotted against the wild folk.

They had gone but a little way farther when a great noise of scrambling and struggling, just ahead, brought them to a sudden stop. It was a mysterious and daunting sound, as if some strong creatures were fighting, voicelessly, to the death. With the utmost stealth they crept forward, along the snow-shoe trail, and came suddenly upon a terrifying spectacle.

Here the trapper had set a strong snare of copper wire, baiting it with a dead rabbit, which crouched in lifelike attitude just behind it, under a bush. A huge lynx, rash with hunger, came slinking by and saw the rabbit. Straight through the snare he saw the apparently heedless victim; but he did not see the slender, bright loop faintly gleaming among the green fir-twigs. Stealthily, noiselessly as a shadow, crouching low, his great round eyes coldly aflame, he crept up till within springing distance. Then, his mighty and unerring spring! His huge paws, all their claws extended, clutched the dead rabbit. But at the same instant a terrible grip clutched his own throat chokingly.

Forgetting his prize, the big cat sprang violently aside, with a spitting screech of terror. At the first jump, he saw no sign of his foe, though that clutch was still on his throat. His natural courage turned to water at the mystery of the attack. But at the second leap his neck was jerked savagely, the grip on his throat tightened so that he could not screech again, and the enemy came into view, jumping at him. To his horror it was only a harmless-looking stick of white birch, such as he had seen many and many a time lying around the camps of the lumbermen. He could not understand the appalling and malignant hostility which it now displayed towards him.

First he tried flight, but the stick came jumping after him, clutching the harder the harder he tried to escape. Then in the madness of his fear he wheeled and pounced upon it, tearing at it with tooth and claw. The stick lay quiet enough under this assault, making no visible resistance, but all the while, in some awful way, managing to keep up the pressure on his throat. The lynx sat down and stared, his eyes starting from his head, his red jaws open in the struggle for breath.

It was at this time the foxes came up, and crouched behind a bush, their bright eyes watching and wondering. They hated the lynx; but this inexplicable attack upon him awed and terrified them, as the manifestation of a hostile force which they could not comprehend.

The slender noose was now drawn close, deep in the fur behind the lynx's jaws; and the pressure clouded his wild cunning. A wiser animal than the lynx would have found his wisdom fail him in such crisis. Nevertheless, in his despair he thought of something else to do, a pathetic device. Perhaps the stick was like a dog, and could not climb a tree. He ran up the nearest tree; the the stick followed, tightening, ever tightening that strangle grip upon his throat. He crept out on a great branch; and saw the stick dangling below him. The winter world, the moonlight and the snow and the black trunks of the trees, were now reeling before his eyes, and his swelling tongue stuck out beyond his jaws. In the extremity of his horror he gave one more look downward at the dancing stick, then sprang outward, on the other side of the branch.

As he sprang the stick flew violently upward. It caught under the branch, and held fast for a moment, checking the victim's leap and tightening the noose to its utmost. Kicking and writhing, the miserable animal swung widely to the other side of the branch, and back again. At the top of that backward swing the stick slipped over the branch and the two came down upon the snow together. The stick fell on the lynx's body; and the lynx, after a few convulsive twitches, lay quite still.

Not till the stillness had lasted a long time, and the moon was beginning to sink among the tree tops, did the two foxes dare to come forward and investigate. They satisfied themselves at once that the lynx was dead, then, sniffing shrewdly at the noose and cord and stick, all with the dangerous taint of man strong upon them, they achieved a pretty clear understanding of the affair. This, plainly, was another form of trap, another manifestation of man's tireless and inescapable enmity. It was to both, and to the inquiring Red Fox in particular, a priceless lesson in the need of untiring vigilance.

For two or three hours more the two foxes stuck to the trapper's trail, Red Fox being moved the more by his antagonism to Jabe Smith, and eager to thwart him at as many points as possible. Whenever they came to a point where the snow-shoe had halted, they cautiously smelt about for a trap, whether there was any bait in view or not. Four more traps they found, and left uncovered, as they had the first, to the scorn of such wild creatures as might pass. One more snare, also, they found; but this they did not know what to do with. They were afraid to go near it; so they contented themselves with trampling and defiling the snow all around it, in a way that would serve as ample warning to any creature not hopelessly besotted in folly.

By this time they were once more hungry, and the she fox was ready to turn to her hunting. But the snow-shoe trail still led forward, ever deeper into the wilds; and Red Fox was unwilling to relinquish it. His will prevailed, and the two continued their journey. But at the next trap his persistence met its reward. The trap had been set beside an open spring, whose bubbling waters defied all frost. In the trap a mink was held, caught by both its front feet. The captive was still alive, and bared its teeth at them, dauntless in the face of doom. But the foxes were no philanthropists; and their hostility to the trapper, their general sympathy with the wild creatures in their contest with the trapper, had no tendency to make them sentimental when they found a square meal thus ready to hand. With healthy zest they fell upon the unfortunate mink, who was in no position to put up a fight; and in a few minutes there was nothing left for the trapper but the tail and feet.

The wild creatures, as a rule – and even one so intelligent as the fox – are apt to be whimsical and not hold long to one purpose. By this time Red Fox had rather lost interest in following up the trail of the snow-shoes. Having well supped, he grew tired of investigation, and his desires turned homeward towards the den in the bank. His mate he neglected to consult. But she followed his caprice promptly, with no thought of protest or petulance.

By this time the moonlight was greying into the bitter midwinter dawn; and at that coldest hour of the twenty-four the trees were snapping sharply under the intense frost. The two foxes retraced their steps more rapidly and less cautiously than they had come, carefully observing and carefully avoiding each uncovered trap as they came to it. But when they reached the dead lynx they stopped abruptly, shrank back with a guilty air, and swerved off from the trail. There beside the huddled, pathetic body stood another of the big, grey, shadowy-looking cats, who glared and spat savagely at them. They had no wish to challenge the stranger, so they made a wide, respectful detour, and struck the trail again some hundred yards or so farther on.

And now they approached the first trap. They would look at it again, with that half-scornful, half-fearful interest which their experiences of the night had taught them, then dash home by the shortest path to sleep away the brightening hours of morning. But they found that another of the wood folk was interested in that trap. A big porcupine was just ahead of them.

The porcupine glanced at them scornfully from under his bristling defences, erected his quills as a hint that they had better mind their own business, and resumed his examination of the trap. The foxes knew better than to meddle with him, though they regarded him with some contempt as a blundering fool, more than likely to get himself into mischief. They sat down on their tails a dozen feet away, and watched with dispassionate interest to see what was going to happen.

The porcupine, with a little fretting grunt of disapproving curiosity, sniffed all around the trap, yet managed, by sheer luck, not to spring it. The critical part of the mechanism was, of course, in the centre, where the foxes had left a covering of snow. Snow was not interesting to the porcupine, so, most fortunately for himself, he did not investigate. Had he done so, he would have been caught by the nose in those powerful jaws of steel, and died miserably. As it was, he sniffed only at the exposed parts. They were not good to eat, so to him they were useless. He turned contemptuously, and flouted the worthless thing with a flick of his tail.

Now, as it chanced, that strenuous tail of his, a most effective weapon of defence, struck fair in the centre of the trap, and the spring was instantly released. The steel jaws caught the tail fairly by the middle, crunching through fur and quills right to the bone.

With a squeal of terror the porcupine jumped into the air, but the tough tail held. In his panic for an instant his quills all lay down flat, till he seemed to shrink to half his size, and looked as if he had been soaked and dragged through a knot-hole. Then he bristled up again, still squealing with pain and anger, and turned to bite furiously at the presumptuous instrument. As to biting, however, and things biteable, he was an authority, the best in all the forest; so he soon realized that it was no use trying to bite the thing that had him by the tail. Thereupon he started to drag it away. The trap yielded and moved a few feet; then stopped resolutely. It was chained to the foot of a bush.

The porcupine, however, is the most obstinate of animals, and, having started, he was not likely to be stopped. If it was his tail that tried to stop him, so much worse for his tail. He dug his powerful claws into the snow, and tugged, and jerked, and strained; till suddenly the tail gave up the struggle and peeled off. He went ploughing forward on his nose with a squeal of pain, leaving a great tuft of fur and quills sticking up in the jaws of the trap. Thoroughly frightened, demoralized, and humiliated, he scurried at his best speed to the nearest hemlock, the raw stump of his tail standing out stiffly behind him. Up the tree he clambered in haste, with a great rattling of his claws on the hard, scaly bark, and tried to hide his shame in the highest crotch.

Interested and greatly excited over the affair, the two foxes had sprung forward when he jerked himself free, and followed at his heels till he ran up the hemlock. They did not dare to touch him, however, or even to come within two or three feet of him, so keen was their dread of his quills. While they stood looking up at his bleeding but ludicrous figure as he climbed, they caught a clear jangling of sled-bells through the trees, and whisked behind some thick bushes to watch what was coming.

It chanced that that morning, at the very first hint of greyness in the sky, Jabe Smith had set out with sled and team to carry some supplies – cornmeal and flour and salt pork and dried apples – to one of the lumber camps at the head of the valley. Along with him he had taken the Boy, because he was interesting company. The Boy and Jabe Smith had widely divergent views as to the rights and the feelings of the wild kindreds; but they were both keenly interested in woodcraft, and delighted in comparing notes. The Boy called Jabe Smith 'cruel'; and Jabe Smith called the Boy 'chicken-hearted'; but they were very good friends for all that. As a matter of fact neither accusation was true. For Jabe was not cruel, but merely eager and relentless in the chase when his blood was up. His was the primitive, unthinking hunter's lust. And towards animals whom he did not regard as game, he was kindly and compassionate enough. As for the Boy, on the other hand, he was sympathetic and hated to give pain; but he was not timid, and there was not a stain of cowardice in his whole make-up.

Suddenly the jangling sled-bells stopped, and the listening foxes, behind their covert, peered out with redoubled solicitude. Said Jabe Smith, as he jumped off and hitched the team to a tree, 'I've got one of my traps set right about here! Let's go an' hev' a look at it!'

Now the Boy didn't like traps, but his interest overshadowed his aversion. He jumped off the sled with alacrity, and, following Jabe's example, slipped on his snow-shoes. Presently the listening foxes heard the peculiar, soft, measured *crunch, crunch* of the snow-shoes drawing near through the trees. When they caught sight of the two human creatures approaching, their anxiety increased, and they slipped back to a yet safer covert; but, as their curiosity was no less than their anxiety, by reason of all these new things of snow-shoes, snares and traps, they took care not to go so far but that they should command a clear view of whatever the newcomers should do. As for Red Fox, his instinctive terror of the tall woodsman was somewhat tempered by seeing him in the company of the Boy.

As soon as he came in sight of the trap, and saw the absurd tuft of fur and quills sticking up in it, the woodsman swore in disgust.

'The varmint,' he growled. 'Meddlin' around where he wasn't wanted! I'll put a bullet through his durned fool head for that! I'm wantin' some quills, anyways!' And he started forward to find the wretched fugitive's tracks.

But the Boy's vivid imagination promptly pictured the suffering of the poor beast, with the red, denuded, smarting stump of a tail.

'Hold on, Jabe!' he cried. 'Don't you think he's punished enough, losing his tail that way? And what's the good of wasting time over an old porcupine, anyway?'

At the same time his keen eyes, much more cunning in discernment than Jabe's, had caught sight of the porcupine, crouched close in the high crotch of the hemlock. As he spoke, he hurried forward and tramped over the fugitive's trail where it led up to the tree and stopped there.

'I'll teach him to monkey with my traps!' cried Jabe, the hunter's fever flushing hot in his veins, so that he ached to kill something. He darted forward eagerly on the mixed trail of the porcupine and the two foxes, overran the indecipherable confusion at the foot of the hemlock, and pursued the double tangle of fox-tracks beyond. The Boy stood and watched him, with wide, non-committal eyes and satisfaction in his heart. He felt amiable enough towards the foxes, but considered that they might very well look out for themselves and take the chances of the wild without his intervention.

The foxes, indeed, were not willing to take any chances at all in their present frame of mind. When they saw that Jabe was actually on their trail, they had no more curiosity left. Bellies close to the snow, their red brushes floating straight out behind them, they flashed off with desperate speed – not homeward, of course, but upward towards the rocky ridges, where they knew they could best elude pursuit. They carefully kept the bushes behind them in line with the enemy; but Jabe saw them as they darted off, and let fly a hurried shot after them. The ball hummed like a hornet close over Red Fox's ears, and chipped a white patch on the side of a brown-trunked maple just ahead, and the fugitives sped more madly than ever.

'This doesn't seem to be your lucky day, Jabe!' said the Boy, gravely derisive. And Jabe, letting slip his grudge against the unfortunate porcupine, silently reloaded his gun and reset the trap.

'I'll git one of them durn foxes yet!' he muttered, all unaware of the part they had played in laying bare his devices.

AFTER this experience with the traps, both Red Fox and his mate grew deeply interested in the work of the trappers wherever they found it. If they came across empty traps, they did their best to spring them, or to make them in some way so conspicuous that none of the wild creatures would be likely to blunder into them. If they found victims in the traps, they promptly fell upon and put them out of their misery, thereby doing themselves a pleasant service and presumably winning the posthumous gratitude of the victims; but if the victims chanced to be lynxes, in that case they exercised discretion and refrained from interfering. When they found snares, however, they were at a loss and felt terrified. They did not understand those almost invisible instruments of death, and were afraid to go near enough to investigate.

At last, however, Red Fox himself dissolved this spell of uncomprehending fear. It came about in this way. One moonless night, when he was trotting homeward noiselessly along the glimmering aisles of the forest, he heard a faint sound of struggling, and stopped short. Creeping aside under the thick fir branches, he saw before him, in the centre of a lane between low bushes, a white rabbit hanging in the air, and kicking silently. The struggling shape moved gently up and down, now almost touching the snow, now a good four feet above it, as the sapling from which the snare was suspended lightly swung and swayed. Red Fox understood the situation at once; and his first impulse was to steal away. But, having satisfied himself by peering and sniffling all about that there was no other trap or snare near by, he let his interest master his apprehension. Creeping nearer and nearer, in narrowing circles, he watched the victim till its struggles came to an end. When it was quite still, a limp little figure of pathetic protest against fate, it hung just about three feet from the snow. Red Fox rose lightly on his hind legs, caught it by the feet with his teeth, and pulled it down. When he let go for a second, it sprang into the air again, as if alive; and he, much startled, jumped backwards about five yards. For nearly a minute the dead rabbit kept bobbing up and down, while Red Fox sat upon his haunches and watched it anxiously. When it was still, he went and pulled it down again. Again he let go; again it sprang bobbing and gyrating into the air; and again he jumped back in alarm. This he repeated four or five times, patiently, till he seemed to have settled the strange problem to his own satisfaction. Then, with resolute deliberation, he pulled the body down once more, and held it firmly with his forepaws while he tried to bite the copper wire from its neck. Finding this a task too great for his teeth, he solved the difficulty by gnawing the head clean off and letting it fly up into the air with the escaping wire. Then, well satisfied with his achievement, he swung the headless body over his back and trotted home to the den on the hillside.

It did not take many such performances as these with the traps and snares to make a lot of noise throughout the Settlements; and though Red Fox's mate played no small part in the depredations, it was Red Fox, by reason of his conspicuous size and colour, who incurred the dangerous distinction. Many ingenious traps were set for his particular benefit – and by no one more assiduously than by Jabe Smith. But Red Fox eluded and derided them all with easy scorn; and all who set themselves out to outwit him got not only their failure for their pains, but also the grave and slightly superior mockery of the Boy, who, ever since the episode of the grape-vine, had regarded the clever animal as being, in a sense, his own property.

Severe though the winter was, a winter of scarcity and suffering for all the kindreds of the wild, Red Fox and his mate now got on very well. The greater the scarcity, the more apt were the wild folk, driven with hunger, to get into the traps; and, consequently, the better fared the two wise foxes. Nevertheless, they occasionally felt the pinch of famine, sharply enough to stimulate their wits. Under such circumstances, however, it was always Red Fox himself whose wits originated new stratagems or solved new problems. These things once done, his mate was apt and wily in following his lead.

Among all the wild folk, the one whom, next to the skunk, Red Fox regarded with most resentment was the porcupine. The skunk filled him with keen aversion, giving him a qualm which tended for the moment to destroy his appetite. But the porcupine he would have liked to eat. He was filled with mingled fury and desire whenever he saw one of these lazy, confident, arrogant little beasts, well fed and fat however fierce the frosts that scourged the forest. But whatever his craving, whatever his indignation, prudence came to his rescue at the soft, dry, menacing rattle of those uplifting and deadly quills. He knew, probably from warnings of his mother while he was a cub, that one of those tiny, slender, black and white quills stuck into his flesh might mean death. Once fixed, it would keep working deeper and deeper in, inexorably; and if it chanced to meet a vital spot in its strange journey – brain, or heart, or liver, or delicate intestine – then farewell to snowy forest corridors and the pleasant light of sun and moon.

For all his dread, however, Red Fox would sometimes experiment a little when he chanced to encounter a porcupine in the open. Perceiving that the bristly animal was quite unprotected on its nose and throat and belly, he would make quick feints at its face, taking care, however, not to go too near. This form of threat always succeeded in upsetting the porcupine's nonchalance. It would either tuck its nose under its belly and roll itself into a ball of menacing spikes, presenting their points in every possible direction, or it would crouch with its face flat down between its fore paws, close as a scallop to a rock, and looking like a gigantic pincushion stuck full of black and white needles.

One day, after a heavy snowfall, when the snow was firm on the surface, yet not crusted, merely packed by its own weight, Red Fox chanced to meet a leisurely porcupine just in the middle of the deep-buried channel of the brook. It happened that he was very hungry, and the plump self-satisfaction of the bristling animal was peculiarly exasperating. At first it paid no attention whatever to his pretended attacks. But at last, when he sprang and snapped his long white teeth within a foot of its nose, it crouched, and covered the threatened nose with an impregnable defence of quills.

Had this particular porcupine elected to roll itself into a ball, its story would have been different, and Red Fox would have missed an experience. He would have trotted off in disgust to seek an easier adventure. But, as it was, a new idea came into his head. Half-crouching, like a playful puppy, three or four feet in front of the cushion of spines, he barked shrilly several times, to let the animal know he was still there. Then, stepping gently around to within a couple of feet of the unconscious beast's flank, he began to burrow swiftly and noiselessly into the soft snow. To his practised paws it was a matter of but few seconds to tunnel under those two feet of unresisting material, and come up right beneath the soft belly of the porcupine. With a squeal of agony, the wretched victim strove to tighten himself into the ball which he had been too overconfident to adopt at the first approach of danger. But it was too late. In a moment the victor's teeth found his heart, and stiffening straight out convulsively, he rolled over on his back. Red Fox made no attempt to carry his trophy home to the den; but for the first time in his life he feasted on fresh porcupine meat. He ate all he could, then, seeing no way of burying the remnant without danger of encountering the quills, he reluctantly left it to whatsoever forest marauder might come by.

This victory over the quills of the porcupine turned the workings of Red Fox's shrewd and busy mind to other possibilities of the snow. He remembered the fat field-mice which he used to catch among the grass roots of the little meadow by the brook. The meadow now lay under a full three feet of undrifted snow, sparkling in the keen and frosty sunlight, flecked here and there with a wind-blown spruce-twig, and here and there patterned with the delicate trail of mink or squirrel or weasel. Hidden though it was, Red Fox knew the meadow was still there – and if the meadow, why not also the mice? One early morning, therefore, when he and his mate were playing on the lilac and saffron surface among the long aerial shadows of the pointed spruces with the half-risen sun behind them, he suddenly stopped play and fell to digging vehemently. His mate watched him, first with surprise, then with some impatience, as she could see no reason for this spasm of industry. Presently she nipped at him, and bounced against his haunches with her dainty fore feet, trying to tempt him back to the game. But he paid no attention whatever, burrowing on down, down, till only his brush was visible, jerking absurdly above the shining surface; while his mate sat a little to one side, ears cocked and mouth half-open, watching for a solution of the puzzle. At length the brush emerged, and Red Fox himself after it. He turned upon her a face ludicrously patched and powdered with snow, but in his jaws was a tuft of dry grass. She sniffed at this trophy inquiringly; and then she understood. That bunch of grass smelled strongly of field-mice.

Having assured himself that she understood, Red Fox dived once more into the hole, and this time disappeared completely. Among the grass roots, where the snow was light, it was easy burrowing. He had chanced upon one of the secret runways which the mice make for themselves in winter, wherein they live safely a secluded and dim-lit life. With his nose close to the runway, he waited motionless for two or three minutes, till a squeak and a rustle told him that one of the little grass-dwellers was coming. Then a snap, lightning-swift, and his jaws closed upon a bunch of dead grass; but inside the bunch of grass was a fat mouse. The prize was a small one, considering the labour it had cost. But, after all, it was a toothsome morsel, the more appetizing for being out of season; and the digging had been fun. Rather proudly Red Fox backed out of the hole and laid the trophy at the feet of his mate, who gobbled it down at once and licked her jaws for more. Red Fox, however, showed no inclination to repeat the venture, so she began to dig for herself with great enthusiasm; but fortune proving unfavourable, she failed to strike a runway, and, after sinking no less than three shafts, she gave up the effort in disgust.

It was about this time that Red Fox discovered an interesting trick of the partridges. One afternoon, just after sunset, when a heavy snow-storm was followed by a clear sky of steel and buff that promised a night of merciless cold, he caught sight of a big cock partridge stepping daintily out to the tip of a naked birch limb. Hidden under a fir-bush, he watched the cunning old bird as it stretched its neck this way and that, apparently scrutinizing the surface of the snow. What it was looking for, Red Fox could not guess; but suddenly, with a mighty whirring of wings, it dived downward on a steep slant, and disappeared in the snow. Extremely interested, as well as excited over the prospect of a capture, Red Fox dashed forward and began to dig madly at the place where the bird had vanished. It was easy digging, of course, and speedily he, too, vanished. But the wary old cock was wide awake, of course; and, hearing the soft tumult of pursuit close behind him, he kept right on, his powerful wing shoulders forcing his way through the feathery mass almost as fast as Red Fox could dig. A moment later, following the fresh scent in the snow, Red Fox emerged, just in time to see the quarry rise and go rocketing off on triumphant wings. Disappointed, and at the same time puzzled, he sat pondering the incident, till he seemed to come to a conclusion as to its meaning. Plainly, the partridge had intended to make its bed for the night deep under the snow, for shelter against the cold that was coming on. Having decided this point to his satisfaction, he devoted the next hour to prowling hither and thither, in the hope of catching another partridge at the same game; but fortune, having seen him fumble one opportunity, would not offer him another that same night.

Two or three days later, when he was returning through the trees in the bitter dawn from an expedition over the ridge towards Ringwaak, he came upon a peculiar-looking depression in the snow. Stopping to sniff at it in his customary spirit of investigation, he detected just the faintest and most elusive scent of partridge. Remembering his recent experience, he understood the situation at once; and he concluded, also, that at this hour the partridge was likely to be not only at home, but sound asleep. Very cautiously and noiselessly he began to dig, pushing the snow out under his belly as softly as the flakes themselves might fall. In a few seconds the scent grew stronger. Then, invisible but just before his nose, there was a sudden flutter. Quick as thought he lunged forward through the smother – and his jaws met in a bunch of warm feathers. There was a blind, fierce, scrambling tussle with unseen, convulsive wings; and the cunning hunter backed forth into the stinging air with his prize. His satisfaction over this capture was more keen than if he had made a dozen kills in the customary way.

As the long winter drew towards an end, there came one night a rain which gradually grew so cold that it froze the instant it fell. In a little while every bush and branch and twig was thickly crusted with crystal, and the surface of the snow overlaid with a coat of transparent armour. Because of this bitter rain, which froze on their fur, the two foxes stayed safe in their den all night. When the weather had cleared and they poked their sharp noses out to investigate, it was after sunrise, and their world had undergone a miraculous transformation. It was radiant, shimmering, rainbow-coloured ice on every side. The open spaces flashed a pink and saffron and lilac sheen, thin and elusive as the tints of dew; while the trees seemed simply to rain splendour, so bewildering were their glories of emerald, rose, and pearl. The two foxes stared in amazement; then, realizing that, for all its strange disguise, this was their own old world after all, and a world in which, no matter what queer things happened, one must eat, they started off in opposite directions to forage, slipping and scrambling as they went, till their feet grew accustomed to the treacherous glare.

Getting a steady foothold at last, Red Fox trotted on alertly, scrutinizing the mysterious glitter in the hope of seeing a rabbit or a squirrel, or some luckless bird frozen to its perch during sleep. He looked everywhere except directly under his feet, where he had no reason to expect anything. A fox, however, is always ready for the unexpected. There is little that can escape his alert vigilance. All at once he became aware of a kind of dark shadow beneath the translucent surface over which he was travelling. He stopped abruptly to investigate. As he did so, the shadow wavered away, and at the same time seemed to shrink down from the surface. Step by step, to this side and to that, he followed, much puzzled; till at length the truth flashed upon him. The elusive shape was a partridge, imprisoned by the icy covering spread over her during her sleep. Of course she could see Red Fox in the same dim, confused way in which he could see her; and she was desperately striving to elude the vague but terrible foe.

Red Fox was much elated by this discovery, and promptly pounced upon the shadow with jaws and fore paws together. But the ice was not only the frightened bird's prison, but its protection as well. Again and again Red Fox strove to break through, but in vain; and at length, angry and baffled, he lay down right over the exhausted prisoner, and tried to think of something to do. Fascinated with fear the partridge stared upward, and panting with eagerness Red Fox glared downward. But that firm film of ice was inflexibly impartial, and hunter and hunted could come no closer.

Glancing about in his disappointment, Red Fox

noticed a dense young fir-tree about ten feet away, with its mat of dark but crystal-covered branches growing down to the ground. This gave him just the idea which his nimble wits were seeking. He remembered that whenever there was a crust on the snow strong enough to bear him up, he nevertheless would break through when he passed under a thick, low-growing tree. Here, then, was his opportunity. Darting over to the young fir, he made a great rattling as he squeezed under the stiff branches and sent the brittle crystals clattering down. Sure enough, the snow under the shelter of the branches was quite soft, and he sank to his belly in it. Giving one glance through the branches to note the direction he must take, he began burrowing his best, and speedily found himself out in the clear, diffused light beneath the ice.

When he had gone about ten feet, he was surprised to find no sight, sound, or scent of the quarry he was pursuing. He kept on a little further, confident that he could not have made any mistake. Then he grew doubtful and changed his direction. Again and again he changed it, circling this way and that, but never a trace of scent or feather was to be found. Reluctantly he realized that in that strange environment his senses and his instinct were alike at fault. He had no idea at all which way he was going.

As this fact dawned upon him, he made a sudden upward surge, thinking to break the ice and regain the free air where his senses would no longer play him false. But, to his amazement, the ice would not yield. Rather, it was the soft snow beneath him which yielded. Again and again he surged upward with all his strength; but he could get no purchase for his strength, and that frail-looking sheet of milky ice was hard as steel. With a qualm of sudden fear, he realized that, for the first time in his life, he was lost – and lost actually in his own woods. Moreover, he was actually a prisoner, caught in such a trap as he had never dreamed of.

There was, of course, plenty of air in his bright prison, for the snow was full of it. Through the ice above his head he could see vague dark shadows amid the sheen, and knew they were the shapes of the nearest trees. Standing quite still for a moment, he pondered the situation carefully. Why, of course, his way out lay wherever those shadows were thickest and blackest. This conclusion entirely eased his dread. Carefully considering the signs which came to him so dimly, he decided that the shadows were most promising straight ahead. Straight ahead, therefore, he pushed his way, keeping his back close against the under surface of the crust. The friendly shadows loomed larger and clearer. He was just at the edge of them, when he found that his was not the only cunning intelligence among the forest kindreds. He came upon the scent of the partridge, which was evidently seeking the same exit. In the trail of the fleeing bird the snow was broken, so that he was able to dart forward swiftly, which he did in the hope of redeeming his discomfiture at the last moment. The scent came strong and fresh. He heard a fluttering just ahead. With a fierce spring he caught a single tail feather in his teeth. Then there was a great whirr of wings, and he burst forth into the air to see the triumphant but badly frightened bird winnowing off beneath the thick branches. Much chagrined, he gazed after her for half a minute, his tongue hanging out and his face bleared with patches of snow. Then he turned away philosophically, and set out to stalk a rabbit through the crystal world.

9 *The Fooling of the Mongrels*

THROUGH the early spring thaws there was little for Red Fox but anxiety and discomfort. He hated the wet, and the slumping snows, and the hunt became a toil rather than a joy. His mate, moreover, being heavy with young, was not inclined to play and wrestle and run races as she had been. She hunted near home, but back among the rocks, of course, and never down towards the valley; and Red Fox brought home to her the larger share of his own captures. For his own part, he now became particularly cautious, never going down into the settlement at all. But he got into the habit of making a long, toilsome journey over the ridge and down into the next valley, and compensating himself for the extra hardships by taking easy toll of the farmyards at the foot of Ringwaak. He calculated that these depredations would never be laid to the charge of a fox living so far away as he.

But in this, as it proved, he was reckoning without allowance for his fame. He wronged his own renown. When the folk under Ringwaak began to feel the attacks of a particularly daring and clever enemy, they immediately thought of the big fox of the neighbouring valley, of whose exploits they had heard such tales. Inquiry in the neighbouring valley revealed the fact that of late nothing had been seen or heard of the notable marauder. From this it was readily inferred that he had shifted his field of operations. Thereupon there were many efforts made to trail the audacious raider back to his lair. But the trail invariably lost itself among rocks and ravines and tumbled thickets before it reached the summit of the ridge. Of traps and snares, of course, scores were set; but these were always treated with contumelious scorn, or else given a wide berth. So it came about at last that a message was sent over to the next valley, asking the farmers to hunt down their troublesome, furry outlaw, or at least keep him at home.

Not without a certain pride did the settlement accept this tribute to Red Fox's prowess. But at the same time it was agreed that something had to be done. The Boy smiled wisely, and said that whatever was done, Red Fox would not be the one to regret it. But Jabe Smith undertook to lead a hunt, with the two dogs, that should end in Red Fox's final discomfiture, or he'd know the reason why.

For some inexplicable reason, just at this juncture Red Fox's anxiety and apprehension increased amazingly. It was as if the stir of hostility down in the valley were conveyed to him by some subtle telepathic force, or as if some inquisitive blue jay, having overheard Jabe Smith's plans, had brought word in an occult way to Red Fox of the mischief brewing against him. Let the scientist, if he will, take the one explanation, and the lover of fairy-tale and fable the other. Or, perhaps, the responsibility of approaching fatherhood sharpened his memory, and he recalled the tragic events which had forced his mother to flee from the lair in the sunny bank. However that may be, one evening, after a fit of aimless restlessness, he ran and sniffed inquiringly about the entrance to the old den, under the juniper-bush. Something which he saw there decided him. Returning to his own lair, half by force and half by coaxing, he succeeded in ejecting his reluctant mate, who was now very near her time, and much averse to quitting such snug quarters. This feat accomplished, he resolutely led her away up to the crest of the ridge, to a sort of rude little cave which he had found in the side of a rocky ravine. This done, and his mate – because she could not help herself or make head against his dominance – apparently reconciled, his restless solicitude vanished. He went back alone to the den in the bank and waited to see what was going to happen. He was now less careful about his hunting-grounds, and permitted himself, in his confidence, to range once more the lower slopes and the fringes of the settlement.

When Jabe Smith was ready for the grand hunt, he bethought him of the old den on the hillside where the fox had been 'dug out' of house and home the previous year. He had not thought of this place before, because he knew that the scene of such tragic discomfiture and defeat would be the very last one that an ordinary fox would choose to live in. But it occurred to him now that Red Fox was no ordinary fox, and might be cunning enough to regard such a place as the safest retreat of all. With the Boy as a critical and unsympathetic, but much interested, spectator, and two young farmers as assistant huntsmen, and the two dogs to do the real work, Jabe Smith led the way to that secluded hole in the bank far up the hillside.

'You'll never find him there, Jabe,' jeered the Boy,

encouragingly, from time to time. And Jabe, having his own misgivings on the subject, maintained a strategic silence.

Within a hundred yards of the bank, however, the dogs, who had been quartering the soft and shrunken snow on every side, suddenly set up a chorus of excited yelpings and bayings. They had come upon a perfect tangle of fox-tracks. Jabe Smith's gaunt face broke into a liberal grin, and turning to the Boy triumphantly, he cried:

'There, now, what did I tell you?'

The two young farmers ran forward in exultant glee, expecting to find Red Fox securely cornered in the hole, and to dig him out at their leisure. But the Boy, though in his heart troubled and surprised, kept an undiscouraged face, and advised the hunters not to crow too soon.

As the dogs were obviously confused by the tangle of trails, Jabe called them straight to the mouth of the old den behind the juniper. They thrust their noses into it eagerly, gave an inquiring sniff, and turned away in scorn. Jabe's face fell; for it was obvious from their manner that no foxes had for a long time lived in that hole. The Boy tried to think of some sarcasm suited to the occasion. But before anything could be said on either side the dogs raced up the bank and set up a joyous chorus at the mouth of another cunningly hidden den.

'*Now*, what did I tell you?' cried Jabe again, with no great variation of vocabulary; and the two young men shouted, 'We've got him this time!' But the Boy, obstinately optimistic, assumed an air of authority, and remarked:

'There's *been* something there. But that doesn't prove it's there now! And you needn't think it'll be Red Fox, anyway!'

'We'll soon find out!' said Jabe Smith, taking some rags from his pocket and proceeding to smear them with a mixture of gunpowder and wet snow.

Having constructed the 'spitting devil' to his satisfaction, he tied it securely to the tip of a slender birch sapling, like a fishing-pole. Then, calling the eager dogs to one side, he lighted the rags, and thrust the blazing, sputtering mass carefully into the hole.

'Ef ther's anything in there, I don't keer if it's a tiger, that's goin' to fetch him out!' said Jabe. As all the onlookers fully agreed with him, there was no reply; but every one waited with eyes fixed intently on the hole. Slowly the sapling worked its way, till it came to a resolute stop at a distance of about ten feet in. Here Jabe turned and twisted it hopefully; but there came forth nothing but volumes of evil-smelling smoke.

The Boy gave a little derisive laugh; and Jabe, dropping the end of the sapling, acknowledged regretfully that there was no fox at home.

'But he was there just a minute ago,' said he, doggedly, 'or the scent wouldn't 'a' been so hot an' the dogs so worked up. An' it's Red Fox himself, or he wouldn't 'a' got away so slick. He's somewhere's 'round, an' we'll git him.' With this he sent the dogs off over the bank, to pick up the trail by which the crafty fugitive had departed.

Red Fox, meanwhile, had been watching the whole scene from that safe little ledge of rock whence he had once before made note of a kindred performance.

This time, however, his feelings were very different. He knew his own powers, and he pretty well understood his opponents; and he realized that as long as he took care to keep out of Jabe Smith's way he had the game in his own hands. With Jabe he would take no chances, but the dogs he would fool to the top of their bent. As for the rest of the party, he was not greatly concerned about them. The Boy he knew was not hostile, and the two young men did not seem woods-wise enough to be dangerous. But there was one thing certain, he did not want the dogs to come sniffing about among the rocks on top of the ridge. He slipped down from his post of observation, and ran a fresh trail down across his old one, towards the lowlands. Five minutes later the dogs were in full cry at his heels, and he could hear the men crashing along clumsily behind.

The running was heavy, deep, moist snow in the woods, and sloppy, sticky turf in the open spaces; but Red Fox knew that these conditions told more severely on his heavy pursuers than on himself. For a time he ran straight on, without doubling or tricks, in order to get the dogs well ahead of the slow-going men. When this was accomplished to his satisfaction, he amused himself for a minute or two with wild, fantastic leaps from trunk to trunk in a patch of felled timber, and then circled back to see what Jabe Smith was doing. He felt it absolutely necessary to know Jabe's tactics in the contest before finally deciding upon his own. In this backward reconnaissance he ran at top speed, and was back within a half-mile of his starting-point while the puzzled dogs were still whimpering about the patch of felled timber. Fast as he ran, however, he kept all his wits about him, speeding through thick underbrush, and never exposing himself to a possible shot from that dreaded firearm of Jabe's. And suddenly, not fifty yards away, he caught sight of Jabe himself, patiently watching a runway.

This sight gave Red Fox a pang of sharp apprehension, so terrible seemed the cunning which led the woodsman to keep watch at that particular spot. And there beside him, sitting on a stump and motionless as the stump, was the Boy. It was just the place where Red Fox *would* have run, under ordinary circumstances, or if he had been an ordinary fox. It was only, indeed, his unsleeping caution that had saved him. Instead of keeping to his runway, he had warily paralleled it at a distance of about fifty yards; and so his cunning had fairly outdone that of the backwoodsman.

Watching his enemies with almost a touch of contempt from his safe hiding, Red Fox lay down for a few minutes' rest. Then, hearing the dogs at last in full cry on his back track, he rose up, stretched himself, gave a yawn that seemed to nearly split his jaws, and stole around behind Jabe and the Boy, whose eyes were now fairly glued to the runway in the momentary expectation of his coming. He yawned again in scorn, ran swiftly back to the door of his den, zigzagged for a couple of minutes in that tangle of tracks just below it, then headed down along the shore of the brook, whose channel was now open wherever the current was swift.

As he ran, his plans took definite shape. His object being to lead the chase far away from the ridge, he had no motive for puzzling his pursuers any more than enough to keep them from pressing him too closely. The brook was too swollen and angry to be easily fordable, except where the ice still lingered in the stretches of dead water. But in one place he crossed it by skilful leaps from rock to rock amid the foam, because he knew that the dogs were less sure-footed than he, and might have some trouble in the crossing. Half a mile farther down, where there was firm ice, he crossed back again, gathering from the voices of his pursuers that they had not found the crossing as difficult as he had hoped they would. Then he put on a burst of speed, and made for a remote little farm on the outskirts of the settlement, where he thought he could give the dogs something to puzzle over while he rested for another long run. Having thoroughly explored every farmyard for a half-score miles about, he knew just which ones had any tactical advantages to offer him.

At the farm in question the chicken-house was a lean-to shed set against the side of the cow-barn. The lower edge of the roof was about four feet from the ground; and beneath it was a small hole leading to a spacious hollow under the floor. From a thicket just outside the farmyard Red Fox took a careful observation to assure himself that there was no one about the premises. The wagon was gone from the shed over on the other side of the well, so he knew the farmer was away. There was no face at the kitchen window. The big grey cat dozed on the door-step. He darted to the hole under the chicken-house, and with some difficulty squeezed himself in.

This feat accomplished, he promptly squeezed himself out again, then, standing in his trail, he made a splendid leap straight into the air, and landed on the sloping roof of the lean-to. From here he ran nimbly

up to the roof of the cow-barn, and down the other side, and across the highroad, and into a field of thick young evergreens. Here he lay down with a sense of security to enjoy a well-earned rest.

It was fully five minutes after this before the dogs arrived, their tongues hanging out. They ran straight to the hole under the chicken-house; and there, in spite of their fatigue, they set up a wild chorus of triumph. They had run the quarry to earth. The hole, however, was so small that they could not force a way in; and the ground all about it was still frozen, so they could not dig an entrance with their claws. The black and white mongrel kept on scratching valiantly, however; while the half-breed hound, keeping his nose close to the foundations, made a swift but careful circuit of the cow-barn, to assure himself that there was no other exit. Had he ranged away from the foundations he would, of course, have picked up the crafty fugitive's trail where he had made a great leap from the roof of the haystack and thence far out into the field. But the hound was methodical and kept close to work; and he came back to his companion, therefore, quite assured that the quarry was there in hiding.

When, some ten minutes later, the hunters came up panting and hot, they were as completely deceived as the dogs. Even the Boy, when he saw there was but one exit, and that guarded by the self-satisfied dogs, was fain to acknowledge that poor Red Fox's sagacity had failed him at last. With the fugitive at last securely cornered, there seemed to be no need of further haste, so a leisurely council of war was held behind the chicken-house, the Boy sorrowfully aloof. At length it was decided that the only thing to do was to stop the hole, then get leave to take up some boards of the hen-house floor.

This extreme measure, however, was not to be carried out. While he was talking about it, Jabe Smith chanced to lean upon the hen-house roof, just at the point where Red Fox had made his cunning leap. It chanced that Jabe's nose, though not so keen as the Boy's, was, nevertheless, capable of detecting the fresh scent of a fox on a surface so propitious as a roof of dry shingles. He sniffed suspiciously, smelled the roof carefully as far up as he could reach, then turned to the Boy with an air of humbly confessing defeat.

'The critter's fooled us ag'in!' said he.

'How? What do you mean?' cried the Boy, with glad incredulity; while the other two stood bewildered.

'He's not in there at all!' said Jabe recovering himself. 'He's gone up yonder over the roof. We'll find his trail all right, somewhere's 'round behind the barn! You watch!'

Ordering the reluctant dogs to follow, he led the way around behind the barn, and then, with shrewd discernment, around the haystack. Here the dogs picked up the trail at once, and were off with savage cries, furious at the way they had been fooled. But as for Jabe, he was filled with a sense of triumph in the very face of defeat. The Boy had said humbly: 'That beats me, Jabe. You know more about them than I do, after all. However did you find out where he'd gone?'

'Why,' said Jabe, shamelessly prevaricating, 'I just thought what would be the very smartest kind of a trick – an' I knowed that was what that red varmint would be up to!'

Red Fox, meanwhile, resting in his covert among the

dense young evergreens, was filled with indignant amazement at hearing the cries of the dogs so soon again on his trail. What had gone wrong with his admirable stratagem? Promptly and properly he laid the blame upon the dreaded Jabe; and his sagacious eyes narrowed with something like apprehension. For a moment he paused, considering anxiously. Then, making a short circle, he doubled back and ran along parallel with the road, keeping himself carefully out of sight, lest he should attract a gunshot. He was heading for the mill-pond at the farther side of the settlement, where a small stream, a tributary of his own brook, had been dammed, and harnessed, and forced to do the grinding and wool-carding of all the Ringwaak region.

Though the stream, at ordinary seasons, was small, the pond it fed was large, and just now, under the stress of the spring thaws, a heavy volume of water was pouring noisily through the open floodgates of the dam. Red Fox's mood was now an ugly one. At no time anything approaching a humanitarian, he now felt a trifle harassed and crowded. If all his pursuers – the dogs, and the men, and the harmless Boy together – had but one neck – a long, slender neck like that of a wild goose – what keen joy it would have given him to put his fine white teeth crunching through it! He was ready to take great risks in the hope of doing some hurt to his persecutors.

The dogs, following a plain trail, with the scent so hot that it hung in the air, were now following close, with the hunters far behind and out of gunshot. When Red Fox reached the edge of the millpond, which was still partly frozen over, he stepped out upon the ice, testing it shrewdly. Then, returning to the shore, he ran on down towards the dam.

For a space of thirty feet or so above the roaring flood-gate the pond was open. The edges of the ice were rapidly rotting away as the water surged up beneath. On the bank above Red Fox hesitated, lagging as if exhausted, and turned as if he were at last brought to bay. Seeing this, the dogs broke into fiercer clamour and rushed forward madly. At last, it seemed, the game was in their hands, and many an old score was to be wiped out.

Not till they were within a dozen paces of him did Red Fox stir. Then, whipping about as if defiance had given way to uncontrollable fear, he darted straight out upon the dangerous ice. Either instinct or a peculiarly shrewd and unerring judgement told him that the ice-fringe above the sluice was strong enough to bear his weight if he went swiftly and smoothly. With the dogs a few yards behind him he sped safely over. The next moment, above the roar of the sluice, came a crunching sound and a startled yelping from the black and white mongrel. Looking over his shoulder with narrowed eyes of triumph, Red Fox saw his enemies in the water, pawing wildly at the rotten edges of the ice, which kept breaking away beneath their struggles.

Past the drenched strugglers the bits of broken ice went streaming, to vanish in the loud turmoil of the fall. Red Fox ran on to the shelter of a bush up the shore, then turned to enjoy his revenge. The dogs were still clutching wildly at the ice, and the treacherous ice still yielding under their clutches. As he watched, a larger piece, some three or four feet square, separated itself under the attack of the black and white mongrel, just as he succeeded in dragging himself out upon it. The next moment it slipped swiftly off with its exhausted passenger, wallowed into the roaring flood-gates, plunged over the fall, and vanished amid the rocks and smother below. With deepest satisfaction Red Fox observed this tragic end of one of his enemies. Then the men came in sight once more, so he crept away stealthily beyond gunshot, and continued his run over towards the hills overlooking the Ottanoonsis Valley. But there was really no need of his running any farther. When the hunters arrived on the bank of the pond the half-breed hound was just dragging himself out of the water, thoroughly cowed. The mongrel was nowhere to be seen, but it was easy to guess what had happened to him. The party halted and looked at each other comprehendingly. Jabe whistled the dejected hound to his feet, and patted his wet head sympathetically.

'I saw Red Fox,' said the Boy, gravely, sorry for the black and white mongrel's fate, 'just slipping into the woods 'way up yonder!'

'Reckon we might's well be gittin' back home!' remarked Jabe, turning on his heels.

It was hours later when Red Fox, weary but elated, got back to the den in the bank, having lingered on the way to stalk a rabbit and refresh his powers. One great menace to his peace for the coming spring had been removed. With the energetic, enthusiastic, and tireless black and white mongrel finally out of the way, he knew that the hound would have little pleasure in following the trails alone. At the den in the bank he sniffed in deep disgust, for the smell of burnt gunpowder still clung rank within it. He easily dragged out the intruding sapling, with the charred remnants of the 'spitting devil' attached to it; but that heavy, choking odour was something he could neither remedy nor endure. Leaving it for time to deal with, he trotted on to the summit of the ridge – to find his small mate lying in her lair with a contented look on her face and a litter of blind red puppies tugging at her teats.

Towards these new arrivals Red Fox was indifferently tolerant. He considered them rather a bore than otherwise; though he knew they were tremendously important, or his mate would not devote herself to them as she did. He established himself on a dry and sheltered ledge just above the den, where he could keep an eye upon its occupants; and if any peril had threatened them, he would have fought to his last gasp in defence of the helpless and apparently useless sprawlers. For several days, however, he had little time to rest at home and ponder the situation, because his mate devoted herself so closely to her new duties that he had to do the hunting for both. It was a long way down into the neighbouring valley and the chicken-yards, which he had come to regard as safe objects of attack; and it chanced that at this season there was a scarcity of rabbits about the ridge. So it came about that Red Fox found himself more strenuously occupied than he had ever been before at any point in his career. At this busy time the fortune of the wilds flung upon him one of his most unpleasant adventures.

One day when he was hunting, not very successfully, down beside the still half-frozen dead-waters, it happened that a little way up the stream a large mink started to trail a rabbit. The mink had been feeding for a time altogether on frogs and fish, and was just now smitten with a craving for red blood. He had just missed catching the rabbit at his first rush; and then, in an obstinate rage at his failure, he had settled down to the chase of the fleet quarry.

For a little the rabbit's tremendous, bounding leaps had all the advantage. But soon she began to tire. She ran around in a circle; and, as soon as her trail began to wheel, her cunning pursuer, knowing just what she would do, cut across the curve – and almost intercepted her. At this narrow escape her poor little heart came near to stopping with terror, as well as with astonishment at the appearance of the dark, snaky foe, in this unexpected quarter. She ran on down the bank of the dead-water with the mink not ten yards behind her. Her terrified eyes, absorbed in the doom that followed, failed to note the form of Red Fox darting across her path just ahead.

Under ordinary circumstances, an ordinary fox would have discreetly ignored both pursued and pursuer, avoiding a dangerous quarrel; for the predatory wild folks, as a rule, do not like to fight unnecessarily. But Red Fox was utterly scornful of any mink as an antagonist; and he was in a hurry. His hunting was not for fun, but for business. Precedents and vested rights were of small concern to him. Crouching in a mass of dead brown fern, he waited for the rabbit to come up. Then, a straight, darting rush – and the fugitive was caught right in the air, in the middle of one of her wild leaps. One despairing squeal, and her neck was bitten through. Then, throwing her over his shoulder, Red Fox started homeward with his easy prize, never deigning to cast a look towards the baffled pursuer.

But in this arrogant confidence, for once, he made a mistake. The big black mink was no coward, and his keen little eyes went red with rage at this insult and injury combined. It was presumption, of course, for him to think of matching himself against the great master fox, feared all through the Ringwaak regions for his strength and craft. But his eyes were now like two glowing points of garnet, and prudence had been burned out of his brain. After a half-second's pause, he darted like a snake behind Red Fox, and bit him through the hind leg.

In wrath and amazement Red Fox dropped his burden and turned upon this presumptuous assailant. But the mink, with one of his lightning-like springs, was already eight or ten feet away, crouching and waiting.

Red Fox covered the distance at one bound – but when he alighted the mink was not there. The snaky black figure, belly to the ground, was crouching eight or ten feet away, eyeing him with a fixed malevolence. Again, and yet again, Red Fox sprang at him, only to be evaded again and again with the like ease. At last he, too, crouched flat, eyeing his foe with keen curiosity for a good half-minute. Then with great deliberation he arose, picked up the dead rabbit, and once more started homeward with the prize.

He had not gone a dozen steps, however, when again, like a swift and deadly shadow, the mink closed in behind him and gave him a terrible, punishing bite in the other hind leg, above the second joint. Had he been less heavily muscled, this attack might have hamstrung him. This time, however, he was on the alert. He wheeled savagely, under the rabbit's body as it were, so that he seemed to throw the latter over his head. But again he was too late. The black assailant was beyond reach of his jaws, again crouching, and waiting, and menacing.

This time Red Fox felt a sense of injury added to his wrath. That last bite hurt him badly. He followed up the mink in a long steady rush; but the latter was too quick for him, too supple in dodging, and, after having chased him for about a hundred yards, he gave up the vain effort. Wheeling abruptly, he ran back to the subject of the quarrel, where it lay sprawling and bloody on the brown earth. And the mink followed him, not five feet behind his heels.

Now Red Fox was puzzled, as he had never before been puzzled in all his life. He could not catch his too active foe. He could not carry off the prize and expose himself, in so doing, to those dangerous assaults in the rear. And he could not acknowledge defeat by relinquishing the prey. Placing one positive fore paw on the rabbit's body, he turned and glared at the mink with eyes narrowed to a slit and a sharp, staccato snarl. He was threatening before he knew what he threatened, but he knew he was going to do something. The mink, nothing daunted, crouched again, in readiness for whatever that something might be.

At length Red Fox's sagacious brain decided to simulate defeat in the hope of luring the foe to closer quarters. The anger died out of his eyes, his tail and the fur of his neck drooped dejectedly; and he became the very picture of cowed abasement as he slowly turned away from the prize and slunk off. Instantly the mink, content with his victory, darted forward and began to feast upon the rabbit's blood. Like lightning Red Fox whipped about, and was back between two breaths. But the mink had not been fooled at all. There he was, ten feet away, glaring red, but licking his narrow jaws, with all his wits about him. Red Fox once more had the prize under his paws, but he was no nearer knowing what to do with it. In a sudden outburst of fury he rushed upon the mink to hunt him down by tiring him out.

For a good five minutes the mad chase went on, up the bank, through the bushes, over rocks and stumps, through the deep woods – but never more than forty or fifty yards distant from the dead rabbit. The mink kept always some ten or fifteen feet ahead of his furious pursuer, and felt quite at ease as to the outcome, because aware that he had the brook at hand as a safe refuge in case of need. If he should find himself getting winded, he would take to the open water or dive under the lingering ice, where Red Fox would be quite incapable of following him. What the end would have been will never be told; for while neither showed any sign of tiring or yielding there came a strange intervention. A black bear came lumbering briskly out of the nearest thicket, and, without so much as an apology to either Red Fox or the mink, helped himself to the rabbit, which he tore to pieces and began to devour with every evidence of good appetite.

The chase stopped short, while both the mink and Red Fox glared indignantly at the giant intruder. Then Red Fox, philosophically concluding that the fight was off, as there was nothing left to fight for, trotted quietly away through the underbrush to seek other game. Time was too precious for him to think of wasting it in a fruitless quarrel.

But the big black mink, as it chanced, was of a different way of thinking. He had wanted that rabbit, which he had earned by clever trailing and persistent chase. He would have had it, had not Red Fox insolently interfered. Now the rabbit was beyond his reach for ever, the bear's great jaws making short work of it. His rage against Red Fox blazed up with fresh heat, and he had no longer any thought but vengeance.

Following cautiously and at some distance, he waited till Red Fox had apparently dismissed him from his mind. Then he slipped up behind once more, and repeated the old attack, springing back, however, more swiftly than before, because his antagonist was no longer hampered with a burden. This time Red Fox was thoroughly startled. He flashed about and made his spring; but, as he expected, he was again too late. His vindictive and implacable little enemy was crouching there as before, just out of reach, his strong tail twitching, his eyes like savage flame. Red Fox was bothered. He sat up on his haunches and gazed at the mink contemplatively. He wanted to hunt, not to fight. And that last bite hurt worst of all.

Presently he made up his mind what to do. Meekly, and with a frightened air, he got up and once more trotted away. But this time he limped painfully, as if one leg was so injured as to be almost useless; and he kept looking backward deprecatingly over his shoulder. Swelling with vindictive triumph, the mink grew less wary, and followed closer, awaiting the chance for another attack. Upon this, Red Fox broke into a feeble run, limping terribly. And closer still came the mink, feeling that revenge was now close at hand. At last, in passing through a rough, tangled thicket of little bushes and dead weeds, Red Fox stumbled forward, and fell. In a flash the mink was upon him, and reached for his throat.

At this instant, however, Red Fox's faintness and feebleness fell from him; and the mink's teeth never gained his throat. They met, indeed, savagely and punishingly enough, near the upper joint of his fore shoulder. But the next moment his long jaws closed over his assailant's slim black loins – closed, and crunched together inexorably. For a second or two the mink writhed and snapped, twisting like a snake. Then, as the long white teeth came together through his backbone, he straightened himself out convulsively, and fell together like a wet rag. Red Fox shook him fiercely for a minute or two, till assured that he was dead past all shamming; then threw him over his shoulder, as he had done the rabbit, and started for the den on the ridge. Tough, stringy, hard-fibred mink-meat was not like rabbit-meat, of course, but there was a good lot of it, and his mate was not in a mood to be over dainty.

11 A Royal Marauder

THE new lair on the ridge, being little more than a cleft in the rock, had been accepted as a mere temporary affair. Near by, however, was a deep and well-drained pocket of dry earth, hard to come at, and surrounded by an expanse of rocky débris where scent would not lie. This was the place the foxes needed for security; and here, as soon as the frost was well out, and the mother fox ready to resume her full share of the hunting, the two dug out a new burrow, which ran far under an overhanging rock. Hither, with great satisfaction, they transferred the bright-eyed, woolly whelps. So secure was the retreat that they were comparatively careless about hiding the entrance or removing the evidences of their occupancy. In a little while the ground about the hole was littered with the skins of rabbits, woodchucks, squirrels, with feathers, and with muskrat tails; while about the old den in the bank below no such remnants had been allowed to collect.

In this difficult retreat Red Fox and his family had few neighbours to intrude upon his privacy. Over the naked ridge-crest the winds blew steadily, sometimes humming to a gale; but they never disturbed the quiet of that deep pocket in the rocks, with its little plot of bright, bare soil where the young foxes played and sunned themselves. No matter what the direction of the wind, no matter from what quarter the driven rain came slanting, the hollow was perfectly protected. On the top of the bare rock which partly overhung it from the north Red Fox would sometimes lie and watch, with eyes half-closed and mouth half-open, the world of green and brown and purple and blue outspread below and around him. Far down, on both sides of the ridge, he would note the farmers of both valleys getting in their crops, and the ceaseless, monotonous toiling of the patient teams. And far over to the eastward he would eye the bold heights of old Ringwaak, with the crow-haunted fir-groves on its flanks, and plan to go foraging over there some day, for sheer restlessness of curiosity.

But though neighbours were few up here, there was one pair on whom Red Fox and his mate looked with strong disapproval, not unmixed with anxiety. On an inaccessible ledge, in a ravine a little way down the other side of the ridge, towards Ringwaak, was the nest of a white-headed eagle. It was a great, untidy, shapeless mass, a cart-load of sticks, as it were, apparently dropped from the skies upon this bare ledge, but in reality so interwoven with each point of rock, and so braced in the crevices, that no tempest could avail to jar its strong foundations. In a hollow in the top of this mass, on a few wisps of dry grass mixed with feathers and fur, huddled two half-naked, fierce-eyed nestlings, their awkward, sprawling, reddish bodies beginning to be sprinkled with short black pin-feathers. All around the outer edges of this huge nest, and on the rocks below it, were the bones of rabbits, and young lambs, and minks, and woodchucks, with claws, and little hoofs, and bills, and feathers, a hideous conglomeration that attested both the appetites of the nestlings and the hunting prowess of the wide-winged, savage-eyed parents.

Of the eagle pair, the larger, who was the female, had her aerial range over Ringwaak, and the chain of lonely lakes the other side of Ringwaak. But the male did all his hunting over the region of the settlements and on towards the Ottanoonsis Valley. Every morning, just after sunrise, his great wings went winnowing mightily just over the crest of the ridge, just over the lofty hollow where Red Fox had his lair. And as the dread shadow, with its sinister rustling of stiff pinions, passed by, the little foxes would shrink back into their den, well taught by their father and mother.

When the weather was fine and dry, it was Red Fox's custom to betake himself, on his return from the night's hunting, to his safe 'lookout' on the rocky summit above the den, and there, resting with his nose on his fore paws, to watch the vast and austere dawn roll up upon the world. Sometimes he brought his prey – when it was something worthwhile, like a weasel or woodchuck or duck or rabbit – up to his lonely place to be devoured at leisure, beyond the solicitude of his mate and the irrepressible whimperings of the puppies. He would lie there in the mystic spreading of the grey transparencies of dawn till the first long fingers of gold light touched his face, and the thin flood of amber and rose washed all over the bald top of the rock. He would watch, with ceaseless interest, the mother eagle swoop down with narrowed wings into the misty shadows of the valley, then mount slowly, questing, along the slopes of Ringwaak, and finally soar high above the peak, a slowly gyrating speck against the young blue. He would watch the male spring into the air resolutely, beat up the near steep, wing low over his rock, and sail majestically down over the valley farms. Later he would see them return to the nest, from any point of the compass as it might chance, sometimes with a big lake trout snatched from the industrious fish-hawks, sometimes with a luckless mallard from the reed-beds southward, sometimes with a long-legged, pathetic white lamb from the rough upland pastures. With keenest interest, and no small appreciation, he would watch the great birds balance themselves, wings half-uplifted, on the edge of the nest, and with terrible beak and claws rend the victim to bloody fragments. He marvelled at the insatiable appetites of those two ugly nestlings, and congratulated himself that his four playful whelps were more comely and less greedy.

One morning when, in the grey of earliest dawn, he climbed to his retreat with a plump woodchuck in his jaws, it chanced he was in no hurry for his meal. Dropping the limp body till he should feel more relish for it, he lay down to rest and contemplate the waking earth. As he lay, the sun rose. The female eagle sailed away towards Ringwaak. The male beat up, and up, high above the ridge, and Red Fox paid no more attention to him, being engrossed in the antics of a porcupine which was swinging in a tree-top far below.

Suddenly he heard a sharp, hissing rush of great wings in the air just above him, and glanced upward astonished. The next instant he felt a buffeting wind, huge wings almost smote him in the face – and the dead woodchuck, not three feet away, was snatched up in clutching talons, and borne off into the air. With a furious snarl he jumped to his feet; but the eagle, with the prize dangling from his claws, was already far out of reach, slanting down majestically towards his nest.

The insolence and daring of this robbery fixed in Red Fox's heart a fierce desire for vengeance. He stole down to the ravine that held the eyrie, and prowled about for hours, seeking a place where he could climb to the ledge. It was quite inaccessible, however; and the eagles, knowing this, looked down upon the prowlings with disdainful serenity. Then he mounted the near-by cliff and peered down directly into the nest. But finding himself still as far off as ever, and the eagles still undisturbed, he gave up the hope of an immediate settlement of his grudge and lay in wait for the chances of the wilderness. He was frank enough, however, in his declaration of war; for whenever the eagle went winging low over his rocky lookout, he would rise and snarl up at him defiantly. The great bird would bend his flight lower, as if to accept this challenge; but having a wise respect for those long jaws and white fangs which the fox displayed so liberally, he took care not to come within their reach.

A few days later, while Red Fox was away hunting down in the valley, the fox-puppies were playing just in the mouth of the den when they saw their slim mother among the rocks. In a puppy-like frolic of welcome they rushed to meet her, feeling secure in her nearness. When they were half-way across the open in front of the den, there came a sudden shadow above them. Like a flash they scattered – all but one, who crouched flat and stared irresolutely. There was a dreadful whistling sound in the air, a pounce of great,

flapping wings and wide-reaching talons, a strangled yelp of terror. And before the mother fox's leap could reach the spot, the red puppy was snatched up and carried away to the beaks of the eaglets.

When he learned about this, Red Fox felt such fury as his philosophic spirit had never known before. He paid another futile visit to the foot of the eagles' rock; and afterward, for days, wasted much time from his hunting in the effort to devise some means of getting at his foe. He followed the eagle's flight and foraging persistently, seeking to be on the spot when the robber made a kill. But the great bird had such a wide range that this effort seemed likely to be a vain one. In whatever region Red Fox lay in wait, in some other would the eagle make his kill. With its immeasurable superiority in power of sight, the royal marauder had no trouble in avoiding his enemy's path, so that Red Fox was under surveillance when he least suspected it.

It was one day when he was not thinking of eagles or of vengeance that Red Fox's opportunity came. It was towards evening, and for a good half-hour he had been quite out of sight, watching for a wary old woodchuck to venture from its hole. As he lay there, patient and moveless, he caught sight of a huge black snake gliding slowly across the open glade. He hesitated, in doubt whether to attack the snake or keep on waiting for the woodchuck. Just then came that whistling sound in the air which he knew so well. The snake heard it, too, and darted towards the nearest tree, which chanced to be a bare young birch sapling. It had barely reached the foot of the tree when the feathered thunderbolt out of the sky fell upon it, clutching it securely with both talons about a foot behind the head.

Easily and effectively had the eagle made his capture; but, when he tried to rise with his prey, his broad wings beat the air in vain. At the instant of attack the snake had whipped a couple of coils of its tail around the young birch-tree, and that desperate grip the eagle could not break. Savagely he picked at the coils, and then at the reptile's head, preparing to take the prize off in sections if necessary.

Red Fox's moment, long looked for and planned for, had come. His rush from cover was straight and low, and swift as a dart; and his jaws caught the eagle a slashing cut on the upper leg. Fox-like, he bit and let go; and the great bird, with a yelp of pain and amazement, whirled about, striking at him furiously with beak and wings. He got one buffet from those wings which knocked him over; and the eagle, willing to shirk the conflict, disengaged his talons from the snake and tried to rise. But in an instant Red Fox was upon him again, reaching up for his neck with a lightning-like ferocity that disconcerted the bird's defence. At such close quarters the bird's wings were ineffective, but his rending beak and steel-like talons found their mark in Red Fox's ruddy coat, which was dyed with crimson in a second.

For most foxes the king of the air would have proved more than a match; but the strength and cleverness of Red Fox put the chance of battle heavily in his favour. In a few seconds he would have had the eagle overborne and helpless, and would have reached his throat in spite of beak and claw. But at this critical moment the bird found an unexpected and undeserved ally. The snake which he had attacked, being desperately wounded, was thrashing about in the effort to get away to some hiding. Red Fox happened to step upon it in the struggle; and instantly, though blindly, it threw a convulsive coil about his hind legs. Angrily he turned, and bit at the constricting coil. And while he was tearing at it, seeking to free himself, the eagle recovered, raised himself with difficulty, and succeeded in flopping up into the air. Bedraggled, bloody, and abjectly humiliated, he went beating over the forest towards home; and Red Fox, fairly well satisfied in spite of the incompleteness of his victory, proceeded to refresh himself by a hearty meal of snake. He felt reasonably certain that the big eagle would give both himself and his family a wide berth in the future.

AFTER this humiliating chastisement the great eagle flew no more over Red Fox's lookout, but went sailing down his ravine a good half-mile before mounting to cross the ridge. The young foxes, relieved from the only peril that had ever seriously threatened them, played now with perfect freedom all about their high, secluded demesne, and grew visibly from day to day, as the ardent Ringwaak spring grew into summer. By the time June came in, and all the world spread out below the lookout had grown to a sea of vivid greens shading off into shadowy purples towards the sky-line, the puppies were almost able to take care of themselves, and were making rapid progress with their hunting lessons under the careful guidance of their mother. They were lively and impudent youngsters, restless, inquisitive, and given to taking reckless liberties with their self-contained little mother. Of one creature alone did they stand in awe, and that was Red Fox, who hardly seemed aware of their existence as long as no danger threatened them.

One day about mid-June, however, there came a danger against which all Red Fox's strength and craft were powerless. It was about eleven o'clock, of a hot, sweet day when the only breeze that stirred was a scented air caressing the bare summit of the ridge. It was as if the fields, and woods, and gardens, sleeping in the broad sun, breathed up all their savours of balsam fir, buckwheat, and clover gratefully to the sky. About the den mouth, in the shadow, lay the mother and the puppies, stretched out in lax and secure abandon; while Red Fox, just a couple of feet below the top of his lookout, lay in a patch of tiny shade and got all the coolness to be found this side of Ringwaak.

About this time, down in Jabe Smith's garden in the valley, there was an expectant excitement among the bees. Jabe was the possessor of three hives – old-fashioned box affairs, one white, one light blue, and one yellow, so painted with the idea of helping the bees to recognize their respective abodes. About the thresholds of the blue hive and the white hive hung a few slender festoons of bees, driven out by the heat, while in the doorways a double line of toilers stood with heads down and swiftly whirring wings, ventilating the waxen treasures and the precious brood combs within. From each of these doorways extended, slanting upward, a diverging stream, the diligent gatherers of honey and pollen, going and coming upon their fragrant business.

But from the doorway of the yellow hive went no stream of busy workers. Instead of that, almost all the colony, except the faithful members who were occupied in feeding the larvae, or ventilating and cleaning the combs, were gathered in glistening dark clusters over the front of the hive. The front was covered, to a depth of an inch or more, three-quarters of the way up, and from the ledge before the entrance hung a huge inverted cone of bees, clinging firmly together. The hive was about to swarm. It had prospered, and multiplied, and grown overfull. There were throngs of young workers, moreover, just ready to emerge full grown from their cells and take up the business and duties of the hive. It was time for a migration. It was time that a strong colony should go forth, to leave room for the newcomers about to appear, and to carry the traditions of sweetness, order, and industry to other surroundings. Meanwhile nothing but the most necessary hive-work could go on, for everyone was athrill with expectation. Even Jabe Smith, watching from the other side of the garden fence, was keenly expectant. He looked for a very fine swarm from that populous commonwealth; and he had a nice new hive, pale pink outside and fresh rubbed with honey-water inside, to offer to the emigrants as their new home.

Presently there was a louder buzzing within the yellow hive, and an electric shock went through the waiting clusters outside. Among the combs might be heard a series of tiny, angry squeaks, as the queen bee sought to sting to death her young rivals still imprisoned in their waxen cells, and was respectfully but firmly restrained by her attendants. Foiled in these amiable intentions, the long, slim, dark queen at last rushed excitedly to the door, darted out through the clusters, and sprang into the air. In a moment, like foam before a great wind, the black clusters melted away; and the air above the bean-patch and the currant-bushes was suddenly thick with whirling, wildly humming bees, the migrating queen at their centre.

Attentuated to the transparency almost of a cloud, yet held together by a strange cohesion, like a nebula soon to condense into a world, the swarm, revolving about its own mystic centre, moved slowly across the garden, across the blue-flowered flax-field, and halted, enveloping a wide-limbed apple-tree. Jabe Smith, who had followed at a discreet distance, was delighted at this, because an accessible low-growing tree like the apple made the hiving of the swarm an easy task.

Yes, the swarm was settling in the apple-tree. Near the base of one of the main limbs a dark cluster began to form. Rapidly it grew, the encircling cloud as rapidly shrinking. Soon it was as large as a water-bucket. The humming, revolving nebula had condensed, and hung, a new world, in the firmament of apple-green shade.

The moment the swarm was thoroughly settled, Jabe Smith came hurrying across the field with the new hive, a short ladder, and some rope. Planting the ladder carefully against the trunk, he climbed into the tree with the hive, lowered it just over the cluster of bees, and roped it firmly in that position. All his movements were firm, slow, gentle, and confident – such movements as the bees seem to understand and trust. When he had the hive fixed to his satisfaction, so that the swarm could not fail to perceive what a convenient and attractive home it would make, he descended. A few bees had hummed about his head inquiringly. Several had alighted on his bare hands and face. But not one had offered to sting. The gaunt backwoodsman was *persona grata* to the bees.

In at least nine cases out of ten, Jabe Smith's just expectations would have been realized. The bees would soon have moved up from the apple-tree limb to the cool, sweet, dark cavity above them, and taken possession. Then, Jabe would have covered the hive with a sheet, for further privacy, and left the swarm alone till evening. After dark he would have undone the rope, softly lowered the hive, fitted it to its floor – a square of smoothed board with hooks at the sides – and carried the swarm to its waiting stand beside the other hives, where it would have settled down to its business of making honey and increasing its population.

But this swarm, as it chanced, was one with a prearranged plan which it would not be seduced from carrying out. Every now and then the keeper of bees comes across such a swarm, obstinate explorers and pioneers, determined to throw off the ancient domination of man. A few bees did, indeed, crawl up into the empty hive and taste the sweets with which it had been flavoured. But all at once the swarm rose. The cluster melted – and the swarm was again revolving in the air. With bitter disappointment, but knowing himself helpless to prevent, Jabe leaned on the snake fence, and watched the whirling cloud drift off, higher and higher, towards the wood and the ragged slope. Long before it was half-way up the hillside he had lost sight of it, and had turned back regretfully to his hoeing. He knew very well it was useless to pursue that high-flying swarm, which had evidently sent out explorers some days ahead and chosen itself a new dwelling-place in the deep of the wilds.

The day being such a windless one, and clear, with no menace of storm, it was safe for the migrating bees to undertake a long journey. In a little while Red Fox, from his post of vantage, saw the strange cloud moving slowly up the slopes, well above the tree-tops. He knew it was a swarm of bees; for more than once, from a secure covert, he had watched such a swarm with keen interest and curiosity. But he had no apprehensions as he gazed down on the strange flight. He had never seen any bees about these high regions of the ridge and felt sure the swarm was bound for some hollow tree or crevice below him. Had he known, however, that during the past few days a few straggling bees had visited the ridge top, exploring the dry recesses, he might have viewed the approaching flight with a certain anxiety to emphasize his interest. But had he known that the tiny, solitary, insignificant explorers had even visited his own den, and found it a marvel of security alike from wet and frost and foes, his philosophic confidence would have vanished. Nearer and nearer came the whirling cloud, larger and larger, blacker and blacker, till now its humming thrilled Red Fox's ears. Before he realized how rapid was its flight, the skirmishes of the vanguard were buzzing about his ears. He concluded that they were going to cross the ridge. For a second or two he crouched flat. Then he felt a hot sting on his ear. Too wise to retaliate, he shook his head, slipped nervously down the rock, and dodged into the burrow. The little hollow before the entrance was already humming with the fringes of the swarm; so the mother fox and the young ones understood at once that there was trouble afoot and that it was time to run to earth. The young ones, however, as they followed their mother, obeyed their natural impulse to snap at these impertinent flies that were buzzing about their ears. They promptly got stung, of course, and darted in with a chorus of yelps, their pretty brushes drooping with consternation.

Once inside, the whole family crouched down behind Red Fox, wondering apprehensively what was going to happen. They were not left long in suspense. Red Fox saw the entrance darken, as the bees gathered thickly down to it. He felt the first intruders crawling in his fur. He felt two or three stings. The puppies began to yelp again. With a sharp bark, which was a signal to his mate to follow with the young ones, he darted out into the daylight, his red coat literally black with the invaders. Still, he was too wise to fight back; and, as the bees were mostly full of honey, and not in a particularly warlike mood, he got but two or three more stings.

Close at his heels came the puppies; and he was careful not to run so fast as to leave them behind. At the tail of the procession came the slim mother, so covered with the crawling black invaders as to be almost unrecognizable for a fox. Quick to learn, she was following her mate's self-restraint, and making no fight; and few of the bees, therefore, were attacking her. She had some stings, to be sure; but most of the bees that were crawling over her were perfectly good-natured, and treated her merely as something convenient to light upon. The puppies, however, were not faring so well. True to their fighting pedigree, they snapped and bit at their assailants as they ran, yelping with pain and astonishment, but not cowed even in this moment of disastrous retreat.

At a few paces from the mouth of the den the majority of the bees that blackened the fur of Red Fox and his mate arose into the air and hummed off eagerly to rejoin their queen in the hole. But those upon the rash puppies, thoroughly stirred up, stuck to the battle. Red Fox understood the situation; and, fortunately for the youngsters, knew just what to do. Darting among the rocks, he led the unhappy procession to the nearest juniper thicket, and plunged straight into it. When the family emerged on the other side of the thicket, their coats had all resumed their proper colour; for few indeed were the bees that succeeded in resisting the firm and harsh brushes of the juniper. Many of them were killed, and many more maimed; while for some minutes the thicket was all a-buzz with those who had escaped injury in the unceremonious brushing.

From the juniper thicket Red Fox led down through a thick blueberry scrub, and thence through every kind of brushy bush he saw, till there was not a bee left in the fur of any member of the family. All the while he was heading for the little hillside meadow by the brook, where he was wont to catch mice. Along the edges of the brook, between grass and water, was a space of moist and naked earth. Here he taught the unhappy young ones to nose and wallow and roll themselves, till the cooling and healing soil was plastered all over them and rubbed deep into the very roots of their fur. Assuaging the fiery anguish and drawing the acrid poison from every tiny wound, the wet earth did its work, and after a time the sufferers felt better. Then they spent hours rolling in the sweet grass to clean and dry their fur; and when this was accomplished, there was the meadow, with all the mice, to afford them an easy meal. Just above the meadow, where the earth sloped upward and became dry and sandy, they found an old woodchuck burrow; and here, for the moment, they took up their abode till a more satisfactory dwelling might be found.

13 *The Yellow Thirst*

THE old woodchuck hole – it was one whose owner had been killed by Red Fox himself earlier in the season – served very well, when enlarged, for the rest of the summer. Red Fox did not occupy it, objecting as he did to the restlessness of the puppies, and preferring the spicy air beneath some thick spruce or fir near at hand. The puppies, with their increasing size and independence of spirit, were by this time growing troublesome to their mother, who had a busy time keeping them out of scrapes. The reputation of their father had secured them against many of the perils which beset young foxdom; and, except for the one little victim snatched away by the eagle, their number was not diminished. Never meddling, never teaching, never disciplining, apparently unaware, indeed, of their existence, Red Fox stood behind the little family and watched that it came to no more hurt. Why he did this it would have puzzled him to decide, had the question in any way occurred to him. He would have concluded, probably, that it was all for the sake of the slim red mate; though back of this motive, without any doubt, the deeper instinct of fatherhood was at work.

The little foxes were now given to stealing off at twilight, or by moonlight, studying for themselves the mysteries of the trails; and sometimes, though not always, unknown to the young adventurers, Red Fox would manage to conduct his own hunting in the near neighbourhood. More than once his wisdom was justified by the event.

One day, as he was lying in wait in a clump of weeds for a rabbit which he had some reason to expect in the runway before him, he saw a big raccoon go running by on her toes, her big, dark, inquisitive eyes peering into every shadowy place. They detected Red Fox at once, hidden though he thought himself; and Red Fox knew himself discovered, by the change of expression, the sudden narrowing of the pupils, of those strange, restless eyes. The raccoon ran on, however, as if she had seen nothing, and Red Fox never moved. Each knew the other very well, and each had the highest respect for the other's prowess in battle. There was no desire to interfere on either side. Had a fight been forced upon them, Red Fox would unquestionably have come out conqueror, but not without rememberable scars; for all his quick intelligence would have been needed, in addition to his strength and courage, to assure him the victory over so redoubtable an adversary as the big raccoon.

Some ten paces behind their mother ran three little raccoons, evidently in haste to catch up. They did not see Red Fox; and Red Fox, on his part, eyed them quite casually. He allowed himself no thought of how appetizing a morsel one of those fat little coons would be. Out of the corner of one eye, however, he cast a keen glance up along the runway, and noted that the mother raccoon had turned, and was looking backwards, to make quite sure that the great fox would respect the tacit truce that stood between her and him.

No sooner had the group of young coons gone, and disappeared with their mother down the runway, than another of the bright-eyed, bar-faced, ring-tailed little ones came along. He was in no hurry whatever, and seemed to care not a jot how far the rest of his family might get ahead of him. He went loafing along, nosing here and there, and apparently took no thought of all the perils of the wilderness. It may have been mere rash folly on his part, or it may have been the extreme of confidence in his mother's ability to protect him even at long range; but he certainly showed himself lacking in that wholesome apprehensiveness which so helps a wilderness youngster to grow up. Red Fox wrinkled his black nose at the sight of such heedlessness, but had no thought of molesting the unwary traveller.

The little raccoon, however, had hardly got by, when Red Fox caught sight of one of his own irrepressible litter stealing up swiftly on the trail. It was the biggest of the whelps, this one, a particularly sturdy and well-grown youngster, who bid fair to one day rival his father in size and strength. He had none of his father's wisdom, however, or he would not have been following the trail of the whole raccoon family. Red Fox was exasperated at this exhibition of blind, head-long rashness. He saw himself, in a moment, more being drawn into a bloody and altogether unprofitable contention with the big raccoon – perhaps with her mate also. This was not to be endured. Darting from his hiding-place he stood across the runway, and turned a face of censure upon the foolish puppy. The look and attitude, together with a faint murmur of a growl, conveyed plainly enough to the youngster all that was necessary for him to know. Sullen and unconvinced, the youngster shrank back, turned, and went trotting reluctantly homeward, probably telling himself that his father had some hidden motive for his interference. When he had disappeared up the runway, Red Fox turned his head, and saw the big raccoon just vanishing in the other direction. She had been back to look after her dilatory offspring.

A few days later another of the ambitious puppies, starting out about sunset to follow the trails alone, got himself engaged in an enterprise too great for him. Under a rock on the edge of a little grassy, steeply sloping glade, where the red-gold light fell richly through the thin tree-tops along the lower edge, the youngster had found a woodchuck hole. Very proud and aspiring, he crouched beside it like a cat and waited for the occupant to come out. In a few minutes the occupant did come out – grumpy woodchuck with a good appetite, starting out to forage for his bloodless evening meal of herbs and roots. The moment he emerged, the rash young fox pounced upon him, expecting an easy and speedy victory. But the woodchuck was no whit dismayed. His squat, brown body, rather fat and flabby-looking, was in reality a mass of vigorous muscles. His long, gnawing teeth, keen-edged as chisels, were very potent weapons. And there was not a drop of craven blood in his sturdy little heart. With an angry, whistling sort of squeak, he turned savagely upon his assailant and set a deep, punishing grip into his neck.

The young fox was startled, and let go his hold with a short yelp at the unaccustomed pain. He was game, however, and reached straight away for another and more effective hold. He bit and bit, slashing his antagonistic severely; while the woodchuck, satisfied with the grip he had gained, held on like a bulldog, worrying, worrying, worrying. For perhaps three or four minutes the two thrashed around in the rose-lit grass before the hole – the inexperienced puppy working desperately and rapidly tiring himself out, while the crafty old woodchuck held on and saved his breath, biding his opportunity. A minute or two more and he would have had the little fox at his mercy, bewildered and exhausted. But just at this critical point in the fight, when victory was already within his reach, he relaxed his hold, violently shook himself free, and darted like a brown streak into his hole.

The old fighter's cool and watchful eyes had caught sight of Red Fox, slipping swiftly and secretly up along the grassy edge of the glade to his offspring's rescue. Very well did Red Fox know the woodchuck's prowess, and he was not dissatisfied with the fight that the youngster had put up. He licked the youngster's wound approvingly, and then settled himself down by the hole to watch for the woodchuck to come out again. He was willing enough to avenge the youngster's wound and at the same time dine on plump woodchuck. But he waited in vain. This was a woodchuck of experience and craft. Some eight or ten feet away, behind a thick clump of weeds that grew against a log, he had another doorway to his dwelling. Here, with just his nose stuck out, he himself kept watch upon Red Fox, moveless and patient. For a good half-hour Red Fox watched the first hole, while the woodchuck peered forth from the other; and the coloured sunset faded into the greyness of the dewy forest twilight. Then Red Fox, growing tired of inaction, went off on another and less monotonous quest. The woodchuck stayed indoors for a good hour more, then came forth confidently and went about his harmless business, an enemy to none but grass and leaves.

As the summer drew past its full, there crept over all the Ringwaak country a severe and altogether phenomenal drought. For weeks there was no rain, and all day the inexorable sun sucked up the moisture. The streams shrank, the wells in the settlement grew scant and roiled, the forest pools dried up, leaving tangles of coarse, prostrate weeds and ugly spaces of scum-encrusted mud. Under this mud, before it dried, the water insects and larvae and small crustaceans buried themselves in despairing disgust. Many of the frogs followed this wisely temporizing example; while others, more ventursome and impatient, set out on difficult migrations, questing for springs that the drought could not exhaust. The fields down in the valley, but yesterday so richly green with crops, became patched and streaked with sickly greyish yellows. The maples, and poplars, and birches all over the wooded uplands began to take on autumn tints long before their time – but with a dull lack-lustre, instead of the thrilling and transparent autumn brilliancy. Only the great balsam poplars, and elms, and water-ash, growing along the little chain of lakes far down the valley and striking roots far down into the damp, kept their green and defied the parching skies.

With this travail of inanimate nature all the furred and feathered life of the wild suffered in sympathy. The stifling and devitalized air set their nerves on

edge, as it were. They were harassed with a continual vague discomfort, and could not tell what ailed them. Their old occupations and affairs lost interest. They grew peevish, resentful, quarrelsome. Instead of minding each his own business, and quietly getting out of one another's way, they would choose rather to go out of their own way to assert their rights; and so there were frequent unnecessary battles, and bloody feuds sprang up where there had of old been a prudent tolerance and respecting of claims. With certain of the animals, indeed, this state of overtense nerves went the length of a kind of madness, till they would run amuck, and blindly attack creatures whose wrath they could not hope to withstand for a moment. For example, a bear, shuffling sulkily down to seek a wallowing-place in some shrunken pool of the brook, was met by a red-eyed, open-jawed mink, which darted at his nose in a paroxysm of insane fury. The little maniac clung to the big beast's tender snout till he was battered and torn to pieces. Then the bear, injured and furious, hurried on to the brook to bury his bleeding muzzle in the wet mud, for the drawing out of the poison and the assuagement of the pain. The blood of a bear not being very susceptible to such poisons, he was soon none the worse for the strange assault; but some other animals, in a like case, would have probaby found themselves inoculated with the assailant's madness.

Another instance of the sinister influences at work throughout the wilds occurred about this time to the Boy. He was moving in his noiseless fashion along an old, mossy wood-road, his bright eyes taking in every detail of the shadowy world, when he saw a small yellow weasel running directly towards him. Instantly he stopped, stiffened himself to the stillness of a stump, and waited in keen curiosity to see what the weasel was up to. He was not left long in doubt. Almost before he could realize what was happening, the snaky little beast reached his feet, and with gnashing teeth and blazing eyes darted straight up his leg. It had almost gained his throat – its evident object – before he regained his wits enough to strike it to the ground with a blow of his hand. In a flash, however, it was back at him again, with a virulence of malice that filled the Boy's ordinarily gentle soul with rage. As he again dashed it down, this time with all his strength, he sprang forward simultaneously and caught it under his foot as it touched the earth. Then, with a savage satisfaction that amazed himself, he ground the mad beast's life out under his heel. The experience, however, had something fearsome and uncanny about it, which for a few days spoiled his interest in the wilderness. Under the malign spell of the drought, the woods had lost for him their sweet, familiar influence.

One scorching morning somewhat later, when the curse of the yellow thirst had lain upon the land for weeks, Red Fox, looking down from the shade of the juniper-bush, saw a big muskrat climb the bank of the dwindling brook and start straight across the meadow towards the deep woods, where no muskrat in its senses had any business. Red Fox eyed its erratic progress suspiciously. He did not like these beasts that lost their heads and acted as nature never intended them to act. Suddenly, to his angry alarm, he saw the big, headstrong foolhardy member of his litter creep out from the den and steal warily down to intercept the approaching muskrat. The young fox, of course, took every precaution to conceal himself, keeping behind the grass tufts and crawling belly to earth. But the muskrat detected him; and at once, instead of darting, panic-stricken, back to the brook, came straight at him fiercely. Red Fox saw that the muskrat had gone mad, and that a single one of its venomous bites might be fatal to its ignorant young antagonist. Like a red streak he left his lair, and was out across the meadow, coming upon the muskrat a little behind and to one side. So intent were the two as they approached each other that they never saw Red Fox's coming. Another second and they would have been at each other's throats, and nothing but a miracle could have saved the youngster, though he would undoubtedly have killed the muskrat in half a minute. But at this instant Red Fox arrived with an arrowy, straight spring, and his invincible paws caught the muskrat's neck close behind the ears. There was no chance for the mad little animal to bite, or even squeal. One jerk and its neck was broken. Red Fox left the sprawling victim on the ground, and trotted back to his lair under the bush, willing to leave the prize to the youngster who had started out to win it. But the latter, sullenly enraged at what he considered his father's wanton interference, would have nothing more to do with it. He turned off sulkily into the woods, and the body was left neglected in the sun, an object of immediate interest to the ants and flies.

WHEN the drought had grown almost unbearable, and man and beast, herb and tree, all seemed to hold up hands of appeal together to the brazen sky, crying out, 'How long? How long?' there came at last a faint, acrid pungency on the air which made the dry woods shudder with fear. Close on the heels of this fierce, menacing smell came a veil of thinnest vapour, lilac-toned, delicate, magical, and indescribably sinister. Sky and trees, hills and fields, they took on a new beauty under this light, transfiguring touch. But the touch was one that made all the forest folk, and the settlement folk as well, scan the horizon anxiously and calculate the direction of the wind.

Miles away, far down the wooded ridges and beyond the farthest of the little lakes to southward, some irresponsible and misbegotten idiot had gone away and left his camp-fire burning. Eating its way furtively through the punk-dry turf, and moss, and dead-leaf débris, the fire had spread undiscovered over an area of considerable width, and had at last begun to lay hold upon the trees. On an almost imperceptible wind, one morning, the threatening pungency stole up over the settlement and the ridge. Later in the day the thinnest of the smoke-veil arrived. And that night, had anyone been on watch on the top of the ridge, where Red

Fox had had his lookout two months earlier, he might have discerned a thread of red light, cut here and there with slender, sharp tongues of flame, along a section of the southward sky. Only the eagles, however, saw this beautiful, ominous sight. In the last of the twilight they rose and led off their two nestlings – now clothed with loose black feathers, and looking nearly as huge as their parents – to the top of a naked cliff far up the flank of old Ringwaak. Here they all four huddled together on a safe ledge, and watched the disastrous red light with fascinated eyes.

Red Fox, meanwhile, was in his lair, too troubled and apprehensive to go hunting. He had had no experience of that scourge of the drought-stricken woods, the forest fire. His instinct gave him no sufficient information on the subject, at least at this early stage of the emergency. And for once his keen sagacity found itself at fault. He could do nothing but wait.

As the night deepened a wind arose, and the red line across the southern horizon became a fierce glow that mounted into the sky, with leaping spires of flame along its lower edge. The wind quickly grew into a gale, driving the smoke and flame before it. Soon a doe and two fawns, their eyes wide with terror, went bounding past Red Fox. Still he made no stir, for he wanted to know more about the peril that threatened him before he decided which way to flee to escape it. As he pondered – no longer resting under his bush, but standing erect behind his den mouth, his mate and youngsters crouching near and trembling – a clumsy porcupine rattled past, at a pace of which Red Fox would never have believed a porcupine capable. Then a weasel – and four or five rabbits immediately at its heels, all unmindful of its insatiable ferocity. By this time the roar and savage crackle of the flames came clearly down the wind, with puffs of choking smoke. It was plainly time to do something. Red Fox decided that it was hopeless to flee straight ahead of the flames, which would be sure to outrace and outwind his family in a short time. He thought it best to run at a slant across the path of the conflagration, and so, if possible, get beyond the skirts of it. He thought of the open fields adjoining the settlement, and made up his mind that there lay the best chance of safety. With a sharp signal to his mate, he started on a long diagonal across the meadow, over the brook, and down the hill, the whole family keeping close behind him. No sooner had they crossed it than the meadow was suddenly alive with fleeing shapes – deer, and a bear, woodchucks, squirrels, and rabbits, two wildcats, and mice, weasels, and porcupines. There were no muskrats or mink, because these latter were keeping close to the watercourses, however shrunken, and putting their trust in these for final escape.

As Red Fox ran on his cunning cross line, he suddenly saw the red tongues licking through the trees ahead of him, while blazing brands and huge sparks began to drop about him. The air was full of appalling sights and sounds. Seeing that the fire had cut him off, he turned and ran on another diagonal, hoping to escape over the ridge. For a little while he sped thus, cutting across the stream of wild-eyed fugitives but presently found that in this direction also the flames had headed him. Checked straight behind his den by a long stretch of hardwood growth, the flames had gone far ahead on either flank, tearing through the dry balsamy fir and spruce groves. Not understanding the properties of that appalling element, fire, nor guessing that it preferred some kinds of woods to others, Red Fox had been misled in his calculations. There was nothing now for him to do but join the ordinary, panic-stricken throng of fugitives, and flee straight ahead.

In this frightful and uncomprehended situation, however, Red Fox kept his wits about him. He remembered that about a mile ahead, a little lower down, there was a swamp on a kind of hillside plateau, and a fair-sized beaver pond at the farther end of it. Swerving somewhat to the left, he led the way towards this possible refuge, at the utmost speed of which his family were capable. This speed, of course, was regulated by the pace of the weakest members; and for the big, headstrong whelp, whom his father had had to save from the old raccoon and from the mad muskrat, it was by no means fast enough. Terrified, but at the same time independent and self-confident, he darted ahead, neck and neck with a bunch of rabbits and a weasel, none of whom appeared to have the slightest objection to his comapny. To his mother's urgent calls he paid no heed whatever, and in a moment he had vanished. Whether his strength and blind luck pulled him through, or whether he perished miserably, overtaken by the flames, Red Fox never knew.

Keeping very close together, the diminished family sped on, bellies to earth, through the strange, hushed rustle of the silently fleeing wild creatures. Behind them the crackling roar of the fire deepened rapidly, while the dreadful glow of the sky seemed to lean forward as if to topple upon them. From time to time the smoke volleyed thicker about them, as if to strangle and engulf them. Over their heads flew hundreds of panic-blinded birds – grouse, and woodpeckers, and the smaller sparrow and warbler tribes. But the wiser crows, with the hawks and owls, knew enough to fly high into the air beyond the clutch of the flames.

Comparing the speed of his own flight with that of the flames behind him, Red Fox felt that he would make the beaver pond in time, though with nothing to spare. His compact little party was now joined by two raccoons, whose pace seemed to just equal that of the young foxes. For some reason they seemed to recognize a confident leadership in Red Fox, and felt safer in following him than in trusting to their own resources. Yet, unlike most of the fugitives, they appeared to be in no sense panic-stricken. Their big, keen, restless eyes took note of everything, and wore a look of brave self-possession. They were not going to lose in this race of life and death through any failure of theirs to grasp opportunity. Had Red Fox lost his head and done anything to discredit his leadership, they would have promptly parted company with him.

The swift procession of fear surrounding Red Fox and his family was continually changing, though always the same in its headlong, bewildering confusion. Some of the creatures, such as the deer and the rabbits, were swifter than the fox family, and soon left them behind. Once, indeed, a wildly bounding doe, belated somehow, going through the thickets with great leaps of thirty feet from hoof-mark to hoof-mark, brought her sharp hooves down within a hair's breadth of Red Fox's nose, so that he felt himself lucky to have escaped with a whole hide. Others of the animals, on the other hand, were slower than the fox family, and were soon outstripped, to fall back into the galloping vortex whose heat was already searching hungrily under the thickets far ahead. The porcupine, for instance, and the woodchucks, and the skunks – hopeless but self-possessed in the face of fate – could not long keep up the terrible pace, and soon went under. All this tragedy, however, was no concern of Red Fox, who troubled himself not a jot about anyone's business but that of his own family, where his interest, in such a moment as this, began and ended.

Suddenly, to his intense astonishment, he ran plump into a big black bear, who stood motionless in a hollow under a thick-leaved beech-tree. Red Fox could not understand why she was not fleeing like the rest of the world. But, as he swerved aside, he saw behind her, stretched out in utter exhaustion, her two cubs. Then he understood. She had evidently brought her cubs a long way, the little animals running till they could not stumble forward one step more; and now, having exhausted every effort to arouse them and urge them farther, she was awaiting her doom quietly, holding her great black body to shield them as long as possible from the onrush of the flame. The fugitives streamed past her on either side, but she saw none of them, as her eyes, strained with despair, wandered back and forth between the roaring blaze and the prostrate bodies of her cubs.

Red Fox noted with anxiety that his own youngsters were beginning to slacken speed and stumble as they ran, requiring all their watchful mother's efforts to keep them spurred on. But a moment later he caught a red gleam reflected from water just ahead. He smelled the water, too; and the wearying puppies, as they smelled it, were encouraged to a fresh burst of speed. A few seconds more and they were up to their necks in the saving coolness, the two raccoons close beside them, and every kind of forest dweller panting and splashing around them.

Much as they hated the water, the fox family could swim in such an emergency as this; and Red Fox led the way out to the biggest beaver-house, which stood, a ragged dome of sticks and mud, near the centre of the pond. There was trampling and splashing and swimming everywhere, most of the larger animals, the bears and deer, gathering at the farther side of the pond. On several overhanging limbs crouched wildcats and a couple of lynxes, afraid to take to the water, which they abhorred. Amid all the confusion and terrifying sounds, the beavers, usually the shyest of wild creatures, were working imperturbably, paying no heed whatever to the motley throngs scurrying around them. They knew that the long drought had baked the roofs of their houses to a tinder, and now, in a desperate but well-ordered haste, they were covering them with wet mud from the bottom of the pond. They, at least, were going to be safe.

By this time the heat was extreme, and the crackling roar of the flames was almost upon them. Red Fox led his family around to the farther side of the big beaver-house, but himself kept watch where he could see everything. The smoke was now volleying down upon the surface of the pond in great bursts, the water was smitten here and there with red brands that hissed as they fell, and the tongues of flame that ran up the tall trunks of pine and fir seemed to leap bodily into the air in order to set fire to the trees ahead of them. The whole south-eastern sky was now like a wall of molten and blazing copper, stretching to the zenith and about to topple down upon the world. Against it, a last despairing barrier already beginning to crumble, stood black and defiant the water-side fringe of trees.

At last the too frail barrier went down, and the roaring storm of fire broke full upon the pond. In their pain and panic, many of the creatures trampled one another under water. Others, afraid of drowning, were slain by the implacable heat. The fox family, however, well away from the densest and maddest of the crowd, sank their bodies quite under water, just lifting their noses every other second to breathe. Red Fox himself, resolutely curious no matter what the emergency, kept his head above the water as long as possible and dipped it under as briefly as possible, enduring the heat till his eyes felt scorched and his nostrils almost blistered, in order that he might be aware of all that happened. He saw one great lynx, his fur so singed that he looked hardly half his usual size, spring far out into the water with a screech, and never rise again. He saw the other great cats swimming frantically, and clambering out of the unaccustomed element upon the backs of deer and bears, who paid no attention to their strangely unhostile burdens. One huge wildcat, badly scorched, succeeded in reaching the top of a beaver-house, where he crouched snarling and spitting at the flames, while squirrels and chipmunks crowded about him unheeded. Drenched from his plunge, his thick, wet fur seemed to withstand the heat for a time. Then his wits came to his help, and he slunk down into the water again, his eyes staring wide with the very madness of terror.

In a minute or two the flames had raced around both sides of the pond and met again, enclosing the water with a spouting and roaring wall of fire. The rabble of beasts gathered at the farther side now surged frantically back towards the centre of the pond; and Red Fox anxiously made ready to lead his family away from the path of the bedlam mob. But the unhappy creatures, too crushed together to swim, merely trod one another down, and most of them were drowned long before they reached the centre. The bigger and stronger ones, of course, survived the struggle, but of these many presently went down, burned inwardly by the flames they had inhaled; and the assault which Red Fox had dreaded was utterly broken. Only a few stragglers reached the beaver-houses in the centre, where the wet mud was sending up clouds of steam.

The pond was no longer crowded, but looked almost deserted in the furious crimson glow, for all the survivors were either swimming about the centre, diving every other moment to keep their heads from scorching, or else crouched like Red Fox beneath the sheltering element. Only the wise beavers were perfectly content within their water-houses, and the muskrats in their deep holes, and the mink lurking under the swampy overhanging banks.

In a few minutes more the heat palpably diminished, as the underbrush, branches, and smaller trees along the windward shore of the pond burned themselves out in the fierce wind, leaving only the taller trunks to flare and flicker like half-spent torches. The heat from the roaring underbrush of the leeward side, of course, was partly carried away by the wind. Little by little the centre of the conflagration shifted ahead, and the leaping spires of flame moved forward, leaving behind them thick smoke, and red glowing spikes and pillars of hot coal to illuminate the dark. The remnants of the bushes along the shore still snapped with vivid and spiteful sparks, and the thick moss and leaf-mould that matted the forest floor smouldered like glowing peat. As the heat further moderated, many of the animals still left alive tried to go ashore, but only succeeded in burning their feet. Red Fox, too sagacious for such a vain attempt, led his family out upon the top of the beaver-house, and waited philosophically for the awful night to wear away. At last, after hours that seemed like months, the savage glow in the north-western sky began to pale in the approach of dawn, and pure streamers of saffron and tender pink stole out across the dreadful desolation. By noon, though the fire still ate its way in the moss, and the smarting smoke still rose thickly on every side, and here and there the blackened rampikes still flickered fitfully, the ruined woods were cool enough for Red Fox to lead his family through them by picking his way very carefully. Working over towards his right, he came at last, footsore and singed and choked with thirst, to the first of the lower pastures, which had proved too wide for the flames to cross. On the other side of the pasture were woods, still green, shadowy, unscarred. In a sort of ecstacy the foxes sped across the hillocky pasture and plunged into blessed cool.

15 *The Worrying of Red Buck*

ON the heels of the fire came long, drenching rains, which quenched the smouldering moss and stumps, filled the brooks and ponds, and brought back hope and the joy of life to the Ringwaak country. But there remained a cruel black scar across the landscape, along the upper slopes of the ridge, stretching from the region of the lower lakes all the way over into the wild Ottanoonsis Valley. It was a scar which succeeding springs would soften with the balm of bush and weed and leafage, though two generations would hardly avail to efface it. To Red Fox it was a hateful thing because it represented a vast and rich hunting range spoiled. The little meadow, however, had suffered no irreparable damage, because, there being no growth of bushes upon it to feed the fire, the roots of the grass had not been burned out of the soil. Immediately after the rains a fresh young herbage sprang up all over it, from the brook's edge back to the woods, and it lay like a jewel in its brilliancy, the one spot of green young life in the blackened expanses of ruin. Red Fox and his family went back to the den above the meadow, and found it, of course, none the worse. In fact, the desolation surrounding it made it all the more secure from intrusion or discovery. In the course of the next few weeks the young ones, now as large as their mother, and with much of their father's independence of spirit, scattered off to shift for themselves; and Red Fox dropped back with a sense of relief into the pleasant routine of his life before their coming. He visited the farms in the settlement more frequently now than of old, because he knew that the half-breed hound had lost all interest in hunting since the death of his comrade, the black and white mongrel. He kept, of course, a wary lookout to avoid stumbling across Jabe Smith; but with the rest of the settlement and their possessions he did not hesitate to take liberties. Once, indeed, the half-breed hound picked up his hot trail and followed him with some of the old eagerness; but when, tiring of the game, Red Fox turned with bared teeth and stood at bay, the dog remembered urgent business back at the farm, and hurried off to see to it.

For a season now the big fox's daily life, though to himself filled with inexhaustible interest, was not adventurous. His mastery, where mastery was possible, was so assured and recognized, and his few enemies were so well comprehended, that ordinary caution held him secure. He needed, to be sure, at this stage in his career, all the sagacity with which nature and his excellent ancestors had so liberally endowed him; for his unfailing triumphs over circumstances had given him that self-confident pride which so often proves a snare to its possessor.

Along in the last week of September, one evening about sunset, Red Fox was enjoying a good stretch after a nap beneath his juniper-bush, when he saw a tall, high-antlered red buck standing about ten feet away and eyeing him with a kind of hostile curiosity.

It was rutting season, when, as Red Fox knew, the bucks were always looking for trouble. But he also knew that the handsome, arrogant-looking beast could have no possible excuse for a quarrel with him. He finished his stretching unconcernedly, therefore, then sat upon his haunches and stared, good-naturedly enough, at the visitor. What was his surprise, then, when the latter, apparently enraged because the small red animal by the juniper-bush did not seem afraid, suddenly bounded at him with a beautiful graceful ferocity, and struck at him with his keen fore hooves.

Had one of the big black stumps on the hillside pounced upon him, Red Fox could not have been more astonished. His astonishment, however, did not make him lose his wits. He was out of the way like a flash before that murderous hoof descended. But the angry buck followed him up, bounding like a great ball, and striking again and again at the small, brush-tailed creature who so easily eluded him. With each failure he grew more and more irate; but at last, half-winded with the violence of his efforts, he stopped, his great red sides panting. For half a minute he stared at Red Fox irresolutely; while Red Fox sat up on his haunches ten yards off and stared back with an unruffled, indifferent air. Then, apparently concluding that he had made a mistake, the hot-headed animal wheeled daintily and moved off across the meadow.

But he was not to get away so easily. Red Fox's blood was up. The attack had been unprovoked, and altogether senseless. Between the foxes and the deer there had always been a kind of informal peace, their interests in no way conflicting. Red Fox was minded to make the haughty animal suffer for his rashness.

Departing from the custom of his kind, he now slipped forward swiftly – as a dog might, or a solitary wolf in dealing with a moose – and nipped the buck smartly on the hind leg.

Deeply insulted, the buck wheeled about and struck at his presumptuous assailant. But Red Fox was already beyond his reach. After a couple of futile rushes he gave up the effort and again moved away grandly about his business, with an air that seemed to say that foxes, if there were such things, were quite beneath his notice. No sooner had he fairly turned, however, than he felt again Red Fox's long, avenging teeth in his hind leg.

With a little worry mingled in his rage, the buck turned once more. But this time he made but one effort to catch his nimble assailant. Then he stood and eyed Red Fox, shaking his proud antlers and stamping with his fine-edged fore hooves. Thereupon Red Fox ran around him half a dozen times, this way and that in dazzlingly swift circles, which kept the tall animal wheeling nervously in the effort to face him. At last he darted in so cleverly that he got another nip at the buck's hind leg; and the buck, now quite demoralized, made a wild leap into the air, and started away in great leaps, across the meadow, over the brook, and through the burnt woods beyond.

This was a victory to swell even Red Fox's heart with pride – and his mate had been watching it all from the door of her den. The natural and fox-like thing for the victor to have done, now, was to be content with such a triumph. But Red Fox wanted to inflict punishment. Moreover, he had learned a great deal from the persistent trailing of the dogs in the days when the hound and the mongrel had persecuted him. Like a hunting dog, therefore, he set out in pursuit of the fleeing buck, following him by sight through the naked ruins of the woods.

In a very few minutes the buck, somewhat short-winded from his earlier efforts, paused and looked back. In a moment he caught sight of the low, red figure, belly to earth and stretched straight out, coming up upon him swiftly through the blackened stumps. In a panic he ran on again till the pursuer was out of sight. Then again he stopped to take breath, running back a little way, after the custom of his kind, and lying down with his face towards the danger. But he had no more than settled himself, his flanks heaving and his fine nostrils wide, when again the red pursuer came in sight, following implacably. With heart almost bursting, the harassed buck sprang to his feet, and resumed his flight through the trunks and rampikes.

After this had been repeated two or three times, at ever shortening intervals as the fugitive's distress increased, the chase led out of the burnt woods and into the unscarred forest. Here, owing to Red Fox's comparatively indifferent powers of trailing, the buck would have had a great advantage had he been fresh. But instead of that he was now on the verge of utter collapse. Once fairly inside the leafy coverts, he stopped, unable to run a step farther. His legs were trembling so that they could hardly support him, but he turned and stood at bay, ready to make a last fight against the mysterious enemy whom he had so rashly challenged.

A moment more and Red Fox came up. The buck

struck at him frantically, but he kept out of reach, circling, and considering the situation. Then he sat up, about twenty feet away, and coolly eyed the unhappy buck. He noted the starting eyes, the flaring nostrils, the labouring flanks, the quivering knees. The victory was certainly complete, the vengeance surely effective. He did not see exactly what else to do. Though beaten, the big beast was not killed; and Red Fox had no desire to hazard a final mix-up with those desperate hooves. In this novel chase there had been no thought of hunting, but only of wiping out an affront. At last, though with a certain hesitation of manner, Red Fox got up, licked his lips, took a last triumphant look at his discomfited enemy, and trotted away through the underbrush to hunt for a mouse or a rabbit. The buck stared after him for a half a minute, then lay down in his tracks to recover.

16 *In the Hands of the Enemy*

In the meantime, ever since the worsting of the hunters and the death of the black and white mongrel, the fame of Red Fox had been growing throughout the settlements. Few, of course, had seen him; but all had heard of him, and were ready to tell more or less inaccurate stories of his feats of cunning and daring, as well as of his unusual size and remarkable beauty of colour. Innumerable were the tales that were told of vain efforts to shoot or ensnare him. And gradually it had come about that every successful raid of hawk or owl, weasel or wildcat, was laid to the credit of the redoubtable red adventurer. A good story gained tenfold interest if Red Fox was made the hero of it. Active and untiring though he was, he would have needed the faculty of being in ten places at once, to have accomplished half that he was credited with.

As it happened, however, there were perhaps not half a dozen people in the settlement who could boast of having actually seen the famous fox; and there were but two who really knew much about him. These two, of course, by that caprice of fate or affinity which amuses itself by drawing certain creatures often into one another's paths, were Jabe Smith and the Boy. It was interest that drew Red Fox to the Boy. Fear drew him to Jabe Smith. If he came upon Jabe Smith's trail, a fascinated uneasiness usually impelled him to follow it, in order to make sure the mysterious man was not following him. Three or four times had the backwoodsman turned suddenly, feeling that keen eyes were upon him, and had been just in time to catch sight of a red shape fading into the thickets. He began at last to feel that there was something uncanny in this elusive surveillance, some inexplicable enmity that was biding its time. The fear in Red Fox's heart seemed to call up an answering emotion, almost akin, in the heart of his human enemy.

If Red Fox was following the Boy, however, he was likely to meet with a very different experience, one which never failed to puzzle him deeply and pique his curiosity beyond measure. After craftily following the Boy's trail for half an hour, perhaps, through the silent, sun-dappled woods, he would come suddenly upon a moveless grey shape, to his eyes not altogether unlike a stump, sitting beside a stump or against the trunk of a tree. Stiffening himself on the instant into a like immobility, he would eye this mysterious figure with anxious suspicion and the most searching scrutiny. As his gaze adjusted itself, and separated detail from detail (a process which the animals seem to find difficult in the case of objects not in motion), the shape would grow more and more to resemble the Boy. But what he knew so well was the Boy in motion, and there was always, to him, something mysterious and daunting in this utterly moveless figure, of the stillness of stone. Its immobility always, in the end, outwore his own. Then he would move a few steps, always eyeing the grey shape, and trying to understand it better by studying it from a new angle. Little by little circling about, and ever drawing closer and closer, he would presently get around into the wind and catch the scent of the strange, unstirring object. That would end the little drama. The testimony of his nose always seemed to him more intelligible and conclusive than that of his eyes. He would slowly edge away, with dignity and perfect coolness, till some convenient stump or bush intervened to hide him from the view of the grey object. Then he would whisk about and vanish in an eye-wink, dignity all discarded; and for a week or two the Boy's trail would have no attractions for him. But in a vague way he realized that the Boy had held his life in his hands many times, and therefore, manifestly, was not really his foe like Jabe Smith. It was far from his shrewd, considering brain, nevertheless, to trust any human creature, however apparently harmless.

Along in the autumn Jabe Smith took it into his head that it was inconsistent with his reputation as a woodsman to let the wily and audacious fox go any longer triumphant over gun and dog and trap. Having his crops all garnered, and some leisure on his hands, he decided to pit his wits in earnest against the craft of the animal, and call no halt this side of victory.

This resolution the grim backwoodsman, one blue and golden morning, confided half derisively to the Boy, knowing that the latter would strenuously disapprove. Jabe had made up his mind, however; and all the Boy's arguments and pleas left him unmoved. The subject, in its general aspects, had been well thrashed out between them many times, leaving both firm in their own views; but in the particular instance of Red

Fox the backwoodsman felt his position unusually secure. He declared that the more strong and clever the big fox was, the more damage he could do, and therefore the greater the need of catching him. For once, the Boy acknowledged himself vanquished. But the picture which formed itself in his mind, of the splendid, sagacious fox mangled in trap or snare, or torn with shot-wounds, was one he could not contemplate. Though worsted in the discussion, he was not shaken in his resolve to save, at least, the animal's life. He would spar for a compromise. And, indeed, Jabe was so elated at having got the better of his skilful and usually invincible young opponent that he was not far off from the mood to make concessions.

Having yielded the main point, that Red Fox must be captured, the Boy took what backwoods ethics would count fair revenge by casting doubts upon the backwoodsman's ability to carry out the enterprise.

'You think yourself very clever, Jabe!' said he, gravely derisive. 'But *you* can't fool that fox, if you take all winter to it!'

Now it was just on this point that Jabe had his own misgivings. And he was too honest to deny it.

'I kin *shoot* him, for sure,' he answered, unruffled, 'if I take time enough, waitin' and hangin' 'round! Any fool could do that, in the long run, if he hadn't nothin' else to do *but* hang 'round. What I lay out to do, is *trap* the critter, if I kin. If I can't, *you* can't!'

'Oh, you go along, Jabe!' jeered the Boy. 'You can't do it; and you know you can't. But I could, if I would!'

Jabe Smith's long face wrinkled sarcastically, and he bit off a chew of 'black Jack' before replying.

'If you're so blame smart,' said he, at last, 'let's see you do it. It's easy enough to talk.'

This was the very invitation he had been wanting, and the Boy instantly dropped his air of banter.

'I will do it,' he said, seriously. The backwoodsman paused in his chewing, spat over the sawhorse – the two were sitting on the wood-pile in Jabe's yard – and eyed the lad doubtfully. He could not believe that his eloquence had triumphed so overwhelmingly as this speech seemed to imply.

'It's this way, Jabe,' went on the Boy after a few moments of silence. 'I know that fox a sight better than you do! I've watched and studied him; and I've got so that I like him. I could have shot him a dozen times. I know all his kinks. I've lugged him by the hind legs, hanging over my shoulder –'

'The hell you have!' ejaculated the backwoodsman, looking at the Boy with astonishment and growing respect. The two knew each other too well to be incredulous of each other's statements.

'Yes! And even then he fooled me! But I know, now, how to best him if I wanted to. I don't want to. But if you're bound you're a-going to, then I'll chip in with you and show you how, on condition that you spare his life. You'll get the glory, Jabe; and I'll get the fox.'

The backwoodsman spat contemplatively, and rolled the question over in his mind. What he called the Boy's 'durn foolishness' about killing things naturally made him impatient at times, and he was unwilling to seem to humour it. But in this the Boy was certainly meeting him half-way; and he wanted to gratify him.

'What'd you want to do with the critter, after we'd got him?' he inquired at last, suspicious of some strategy.

The Boy smiled comprehendingly.

'Well, I wouldn't let him go again, to give you your trouble all over, Jabe! Don't be scared of that!'

'I ain't skeered of *that*!' protested Jabe, ashamed of having his suspicions penetrated.

'Well,' went on the Boy, 'I'd keep the fox a little while myself, I think, if father didn't mind, and see if I could tame him. He's so clever, maybe he'd not be so hard to tame as other foxes. But I don't expect I could do much with him that way. Foxes all think too much of themselves to let anyone brag of having tamed them. But he's such a beauty that any show or "zoo" would be mighty proud to get him, and would take care to treat him well. I'll sell him, and get a big price for him, Jabe. And we'll divide. He'd better be in a show, Jabe, than dead – whatever some people might say.'

'Don't know about that!' said the woodsman, looking around upon the familiar fields and the old woods glowing in the sunshine. 'I'd ruther be dead than shet up – never to see all this no more!' And he made a sweep with his hand that seemed to caress the sweet and lonely landscape.

'Tut! Jabe!' said the Boy, bluntly. 'Then you've got no imagination. I'll bet Red Fox has lots. I know which he'd choose, anyway, if it was put up to him. So I'm going to choose for him, if you'll agree. Death's the only thing that can't be reconsidered. Why, suppose you were shut up for life, there might come an earthquake some day, and split open your stone walls, and let you walk right out! Speaking for Red Fox, I take the circus. What do you say?'

'All right,' assented the backwoodsman, slowly. 'Only, let's git him, quick! He's fooled us all too long.'

'Do you know,' said the Boy, 'he's a queer beast, that! I've found his tracks about your farm – the most dangerous place in the whole settlement for him – oftener than anywhere else. Haven't you?'

'Of course I hev!' answered the backwoodsman. 'And he's took to follerin' me, in the woods, too. Looks like he had it in for me special. What do you s'pose he's up to?'

'Perhaps he's just particularly scared of you, and so wants to keep an eye on you. Or, maybe, knowing you are already his enemy, he thinks it safer to steal *your* chickens than to risk making other enemies by stealing somebody else's!'

'He ain't got none of mine *yet*!' declared the woodsman with emphasis.

'Then I'll bet it's because he hasn't wanted to,' said the Boy. 'I've seen him looking around your place, and lying in the bushes watching, while the hens caught grasshoppers out in the stubble not ten feet away, where he could grab them without any trouble at all. And I've seen him on his hind legs behind the hen-house looking in through a crack – at some hen on the nest, most likely. If he has spared you, Jabe, it's been just because he chose to. You may be sure of that. He's had some good reason in his wise red noddle.'

'He'd better hurry up, then!' growled Jabe. 'He ain't got much more time to spare. What do you reckon we'd better do, now, to circumvent the varmint?'

'Come along and I'll show you!' said the Boy, leading the way to Jabe's chicken-house.

It happened that the tall backwoodsman had a fancy for good fowls. He had several times sent away for settings of thoroughbred eggs; and having had good luck with them, he had now a very handsome and unusual flock to brag of. To be sure, Buff Cochins and Plymouth Rocks and White Leghorns and Black Minorcas all ran together, and the free mixture of breeds wrought strangely diversified results. But it was a great flock, for all its commingling, and accomplished wonders of egg-laying; and Jabe Smith took pride in having it well housed. The fowl-house was simple, but quite up to date in its pattern, which had been carefully copied from cuts in the *Colonial Farmer*. At each end of the long sunny front was a little entrance cut for the use of the 'biddies', and closed at night by a sliding drop door.

'Here, Jabe,' said the Boy, kicking one of these little doors with his toe, 'is your trap!'

A gleam of instant comprehension flashed into the woodsman's eyes, but he maintained a strategic silence.

'And yonder,' continued the speaker, with a wave of his hand towards the scattered flock, feeding, or scratching, or dusting feathers in the sun – 'is your bait.'

'How's the bait goin' to like it?' asked Jabe.

'Oh, the bait's not going to mind!' said the Boy, cheerfully. 'You just wait and see!'

The problem now was a simple one. The Boy knew that Red Fox had explored the premises thoroughly by night, outside, and would undoubtedly have explored them inside as well but for the fact that nightfall found the doors all closed. He argued that the shrewd animal was expecting to sometime find a door left open by mistake. Now was the time for that mistake to occur. In its simplicity and effectiveness the Boy's plan commanded the backwoodsman's instant acceptance.

Knocking together a little platform of light boards about three feet square, the Boy laid it on the floor just inside one of the small doors. From it he ran a cord up each side of the door, over two nails at the top, and joined them in the centre. Here he rigged a sensitive trigger catch connecting with the loop that held up the sliding door. The edge of the platform he raised about an inch from the floor, attaching it to the trigger in such a way that the slightest additional weight would spring the catch and let the door drop down. This accomplished, with the skilful aid of Jabe Smith and his tools the Boy placed some tiny blocks under the platform to brace it up and prevent it being sprung prematurely by the hens as they passed out and in.

'Now, Jabe,' said the proud strategist as the two stood off and eyed their handiwork, 'all you've got to do is wait till all the hens have gone to roost. Then shut the other door, and take out the props from under the platform. When Red Fox comes, as he's likely to do just about moonrise, he'll be much pleased to find that for once his enemy has forgotten and left a door open. He'll slip right in to see what the hen-house is like inside. The door will drop – and then you have him!'

'But what about the hens?' queried their owner, doubtfully.

'When he finds he's caught, he won't be bothering about hens!' laughed the Boy. Now that he was fairly committed to the venture, the natural, primitive boy within him, which is always something of a wild animal, was beginning to wake up and assert itself. He was growing keen for the event.

That evening the Boy stayed at Jabe Smith's farm for supper. After sundown, when the chickens were all at roost, and high in the pale greenish sky the latest crows were winging homeward to the spruce groves, the trap was set and the other door of the hen-house securely closed. Then in a hayloft opposite, behind the big open window through which the hay was pitched, the Boy and Jabe hid themselves comfortably where they could command a perfect view of whatever might happen. Slowly the light faded out over the farmyard, and the roofs, and the spiky tree-tops along the ridges of the hills. With the cool-smelling twilight came a sort of expectant silence, a hush that seemed to listen consciously; and the two hidden in the hayloft spoke only in a whisper. Up from the stanchions below the loft came startlingly loud the munching of the cattle's jaws on the dry hay and the occasional windy sighs which their great flanks heaved forth from time to time. When a mouse rustled the hay softly at the other side of the loft, the sound seemed abrupt and conspicuous. Then, at last, a change came over the quality of the shadows in the yard below. They grew more liquid and transparent. A silvery glow caught the treetops along the opposite ridge, crept down, and bathed the rich fir masses of the woods in wonder. Then the roof of the hen-house turned silver, and a mysterious, transfiguring illumination seemed to tip down into the yard, making lovely, spectral things of the sawhorse, and the well-sweep, and the cart. Both Jabe and the Boy watched the transformation with wordless delight. The moon was floating up behind the barn.

The radiance had no more than fairly occupied the farmyard, when a shadowy shape came flitting soundlessly around the corner of the hen-house. From the crack in the boarding behind Red Fox had seen that one of the little doors was open. His opportunity – not necessarily to kill chickens, but to explore the inside of the chicken-house – had come at last. He peered in cautiously. There were all the fowls on their perches, sleeping soundly. There was no game-cock among them. He knew these tall, handsome Cochins and Minorcas, haughty but not dangerous. He darted confidently through the opening. The next moment the door dropped, with a sharp rap, behind him, catching and pinching smartly the tip of his beautiful brush.

Like lightning he wheeled about, jerking his tail free. But the door fitted securely in its grooves, so that his furiously scratching claws and desperate teeth could not budge it. In a silent frenzy he darted to the other door. It, too, refused to budge. Then he jumped up, scrambling, towards the window, snubbing his nose against the glass and the sashes. But there was no way out. He stopped, crouched down close beside the treacherous door, and set his shrewd wits working desperately.

The hens, meanwhile, aroused by the dropping of the door, and greatly excited by the prisoner's antics, had set up a wild commotion of squawking and cackling. The cocks were particularly noisy; but unlike the valorous game, they made no move to come down and give battle to the intruder. Their outcry, however, was by no means ineffectual. At the first sound of it the two hiders in the loft swung themselves down, and rushed eagerly to the hen-house.

The main door of the hen-house was at one end. The Boy opened it cautiously, keeping his feet and legs in the opening, while Jabe Smith peered over his head. What they saw brought an exclamation of astonishment from Jabe, and a knowing laugh from the Boy. There on the floor, half in moonlight and half in shadow, lay the great fox, stretched out lifeless in front of the perches, with the cackling fowls all craning long necks down to look at him. The two conspirators stepped inside and shut the door behind them. And the hens moderated their clamour, satisfied that help had come.

The Boy, smiling wisely, waited. But Jabe, after stirring the long, limp body with his toe, picked it up by the tail and examined it critically.

'I swan!' he exclaimed at length, in the voice which one accredits a miracle. 'If he ain't gone an' fell an' plumb broke his neck!'

'Well,' said the Boy, taking from his pocket the small dog-collar and chain which Jabe had lent him. 'I guess I'll take no risks.' And he proceeded to affix the chain and collar. Then he tied the animal's slack, unresisting legs together with a stout cord.

Jabe jeered at him in a dry drawl, but the Boy kept his counsel.

'You never can tell, Jabe!' said he, enigmatically. Red Fox dead is cleverer than most other beasts alive, and something might happen on the way home. He might mend this broken neck of his, you know, suddenly – and then – whizz! – and no more Red Fox!'

'If that 'ere beast ain't a dead one,' averred the backwoodsman, 'I'll eat my old shoe-packs.'

'Don't undertake too much, Jabe,' mocked the Boy. 'You may need those shoe-packs, with winter coming on! If you'll just give me an old oat-sack, now, to wrap this unfortunate victim in, I'll start for home 'fore it gets any later. And maybe if you'll come 'round tomorrow morning you'll find Red Fox holding a soirée in our back yard!'

'Reckon I'll go along with you now,' said Jabe. 'The beast's too queer to let you go alone with him.'

17 *Under Alien Skies*

SECURELY wrapped up in the oat-sack, with just the black tip of his nose sticking out, Red Fox showed never a sign of life during that interminable journey to the home of the Boy. Tucked under the Boy's sturdy young arm he endured the painful grip with unwavering heroism, and never stiffened or twitched a muscle. But if the elated victors had taken it into their heads to peer suddenly into the end of the roll of sacking, past the black nose-tip, they would have caught a shrewd and watchful eye wide open. The captive was not going to lose any point unnecessarily; and peering out into the flooding moonlight he marked well where his captors were carrying him. Bitterness was in his heart as he watched the silvered trees and fields and fences go by – bitterness, and humiliation, and rage, and fear, but by no manner of means despair. Helpless as he was for the moment, he knew that he could not be carried in that way forever. There must come some change. He was full of devices. And he had no idea of counting the great game lost.

When the Boy had unrolled him, and chained him to a staple in the corner of a spacious box-stall in the barn, and undone the bonds that fettered his legs, Red Fox still lay limp, so utterly slack in every sinew that the backwoodsman was more than ever assured that he was dead. To all jibes, however, the Boy answered, merely, 'Come back in the morning and see!' And soon, after having wearied of admiring the rich fur and congratulating themselves on their speedy triumph, the victors went away, fastening the barn door behind them.

From a small window the moonlight came pouring in, lighting the centre of the stall brilliantly and leaving the corners in deep shadow. The moment he knew he was alone the limp shape on the floor awoke to eager life, with a sharp leap that tested the soundness of the chain. Red Fox felt himself violently jerked backwards and thrown off his feet, which sufficed to convince him that the chain was strong. Having assured himself as to its strength, and also as to its length (which was about six feet), he now began to test it minutely with nose and teeth, holding it down between his fore paws and going over every link right up to the staple in the wall. Finding no flaw or weakness anywhere in the cold steel which hurt his teeth, he next set himself to the task of pulling the collar over his head. Backing away he strained and tugged with all his might, but only succeeded in choking himself till his eyes and tongue stuck out. Upon this a memory of the great lynx strangling in the snare came over him, and he stopped abruptly, panting and gasping. As soon as he had recovered from this touch of panic and fully regained his breath, he was seized with a new idea. In the corner of the stall was a heap of chaff and fine straw with a wisp or two of hay. In this he carefully buried a slack section of the chain; and when the work was done he crept away furtively, trusting to leave his obstinate tormentor behind. But when he saw the snaky thing emerge inexorably from its hiding, and felt it once more tug peremptorily at his neck, he seemed to realize the folly of his choice. For a few minutes he sat up on his haunches, and pondered. Then, seeing that for the time there was nothing else to be done, he curled himself up in a corner and resolutely went to sleep.

When, somewhat early in the morning, the Boy came to the stall with a dish of water and a tempting piece of ruddy fresh meat, Red Fox gave him one long look of implacable disdain, retreated with dignity to his corner, and ignored the visit resolutely. He was hungry, and very thirsty; but in the visitor's hated presence he scorned to show either of these needs. When the Boy approached him too closely he would show his white teeth, and a deep, lambent green colour would come into his eyes, almost opaque and seeming like a film drawn over the whole iris. This was a signal meaning 'Keep off!' and the Boy, understanding it very well, obeyed. As soon as he was gone, Red Fox lapped up the water greedily, and fell upon the raw beef. He had no intention of starving himself, but he was not going to give the Boy the satisfaction of watching him eat.

And now began for the unhappy captive four weeks of monotonous vain longing. Twice a day, in the early morning and in the first of the twilight, he would go through his efforts to escape, testing the chain link by link, and then hopefully burying it in the chaff. Only the attempt to pull the collar over his head he never repeated, so great was his horror of strangling. Meanwhile the Boy was unremitting in his efforts to win the confidence of the splendid captive. Dainties to eat, fresh water twice a day, gentle conversation, quiet, gradual advances, all were faithfully and discreetly tried, but all in vain. At the end of the month the scorn in Red Fox's eyes was as clear and uncompromising as ever, his glare as greenly menacing and his teeth as implacably displayed, whenever his gaoler came too near. Then, reluctantly, but on his father's advice, the Boy made up his mind that the tameless captive must be sold.

About this time – for the fame of Red Fox and the story of his capture had spread far beyond the Ringwaak neighbourhoods – a well-dressed stranger appeared at the settlement and asked to see the illustrious fox. The Boy proudly did the honours, and with regret acknowledged his failure to tame the beautiful and sagacious beast. The visitor presently made an offer to buy.

'What do you want him for?' asked the Boy, doubtfully.

The stranger eyed him with care before replying, and understood something of his attitude.

'To sell to some big zoological gardens,' he replied, easily, 'where he'll be thoroughly appreciated.'

Much relieved, the Boy agreed at once, and pocketed a price beyond his wildest hopes. Had he known, however, the purchaser's real purpose, he would have rejected any price with indignation, and even counted upon Jabe Smith's backing in the matter. Red Fox was destined, not for a brilliant 'zoo', where he would be a prisoner, indeed, but pampered and admired, but for the depleted coverts of a Hunt Club in one of the great states farther south, where his strength and cunning might be expected to give phenomenal sport before the hounds should finally tear him to pieces. The backwoodsman as well as the Boy had a kind of primitive horror of the formal sport of fox-hunting, which seemed to them a regulated and long-drawn cruelty. It is probable, however, that if they had consulted the wishes of Red Fox himself, that self-confident and indomitable animal would have elected to go with the stranger, choosing the alien coverts with all their load and appalling perils rather than the hopeless security of the 'zoo'.

As it was, however, everyone was pleased. The Boy and Jabe had their money; and Red Fox, in his open-work, strong-barred crate, was glad of any change that meant getting away from the gloomy box-stall in the barn. Where there was change there might come opportunity; and at least he was once more moving in the moving sun and air.

The journey from Ringwaak settlements to the nearest railway station was some fifteen miles of rough going in an open express wagon which carried the mails. The crate containing Red Fox and his misfortunes was lashed securely on the top of some heavy boxes, so he could command a view of the bright-coloured, russet and crimson world which he was leaving. Curled up on the bottom of the crate, his watchful eyes stared forth intelligently through the bars, missing nothing, but revealing nothing of the emotions astir behind their clear depths. For a little while the road led through familiar woods and fields. Then these grew strange, but the rampiked, ridgy summit of old Ringwaak, his landmark all his life, remained in view. Then the wagon topped a range of steep uplands and dipped into the rugged wilderness valley of the Ottanoonsis, and Ringwaak was hidden from view. Now, for the first time, Red Fox felt himself an alien and an exile utterly. As the granite rocks, and scraggy white birches, and black patches of hemlock, and naked, bleak, dead trunks closed in about the narrow road, the captive felt for the first time that the old range, and the den on the hillside, and his slim red mate, were lost. For a time his faith in his own wits failed him, and he sank his nose between his paws in despair.

After what seemed to the captive, and hardly less to the well-dressed stranger on the seat beside the driver, an interminable age of jolting, the lonely little back-woods station, a mere red-washed shanty, with a tall water-tank near by, was reached. Here the stranger gave Red Fox a drink, and a liberal chunk of fresh meat to amuse himself with, but made no attempt to cultivate his good-will. Unlike the Boy, he had no wish to conciliate or subdue the captive's wildness. At last, after an hour's wait, the train came roaring and clattering down the rails; and Red Fox, in his crate on the platform, shrank back against the bars with starting eyeballs, imagining that the end of all things had come upon the world. When the loud monster had passed him and come to a stop, and he found himself still alive, he was trembling so that he could scarcely stand up; and it seemed a matter of small importance when his crate was thrust into what was evidently a part of the monster, and he was whirled away with sickening motion and bewildering tumult. Not till he had been travelling for nearly a day could he bring himself to eat or drink. Then, little by little, seeing that men lived and were content about him, seeming to have no dread whatever of the monster, he recovered his equanimity and resumed his wonted courage. The process, however, took him another good twenty-four hours, and then, just as he was finding himself master of the situation, the train came to a long stop, and his crate was lifted from the car. Once more he was put into a wagon, and taken for a drive – first through a wilderness of crowding houses set thick together like trees, then through a pleasant country of gardens diffusing into farms, and at last into a rougher region of pasture fields, and swamps, and thick-wooded knolls. Presently the wagon stopped in front of a low, wide-winged, imposing red structure, where men lounged on the spacious porch, and saddled horses stood before the steps. Here the crate was lifted down, and the stranger began enthusiastically pointing out Red Fox's beauties and distinctions to a knot of men who had come forward to inspect the heralded prize. Their admiration was unstinted.

'If he's got bottom to match his beauty,' said one, 'he'll give us the neatest run the "Merrybrooks" have ever had.'

'Look at that cool and cunning eye!' said another. 'He's got brains. He'll give us more than one run, I'm thinking, before that mighty brush hangs on the wall!'

'I could find it in my heart to wish he might fool us altogether!' cried a third. But this foolishly amiable sentiment aroused such a chorus of protest that he hastened to add: 'I mean, of course, that it would be a great thing for our strain of foxes, and therefore for the club, and therefore for sport in general, if this husky Kanuck could have a fair chance to disseminate his breed.'

The suggestion caught several supporters, who proposed that Red Fox should be kept for breeding; but there being a great meet planned for the following Tuesday, just four days ahead, the majority were determined to let the future take care of itself. The last run of the Merrybrook hounds had been something of a fizzle, and now they were not sure there was a fox left in their coverts. They wanted one good run, anyway; and plainly this was the beast to give it to them.

In the middle of the lawn before the club-house the crate was set on its side and the cover removed. On the very instant, as if shot out by a spring, Red Fox leaped forth. Straight before him was a stretch of smooth meadow, leading to a grove of maples and chestnuts. But on the way up the road, on the other side of the club-house, Red Fox had noted a stretch of wild land, wooded and brushy. In the too obvious path to freedom he suspected a snare. The moment his feet touched solid earth he doubled straight back towards the spectators, darted fairly between the legs of one, under the belly of the nearest horse, behind a massive clump of rhododendrons across the road – and vanished before anyone had time to more than look around.

The stranger, who had brought Red Fox so far, glowed with pride.

'Did you ever see such speed?' cried one.

'And such nerve?' cried another.

'He's all right, Mack!' exclaimed several at once.

'If he has any sort of luck,' remarked his first champion, dryly, 'our breed of foxes may get improved, after all!'

THE new land in which Red Fox now found himself established was greatly to his taste, and his blood ran wildly in the sweetness of recovered freedom. He had little time to pine for his grimmer north and the vast woods of Ringwaak. Here were dense coverts, patches of swamp, long, though narrow, stretches of woodland wherein a kind of stiff, primly upright cedar took the place of his well-loved spruce and fir, bright green meadows enclosed with stone walls, and rocky, neglected pastures with snake fences that reminded him of home. Here and there a steep, rocky knoll, set thick with trees which were many of them unfamiliar to him, arose out of the levels; and here and there a much-meandering brook, narrow but deepish, spread out into a pond which suggested to him a plenitude of wild ducks. From a rock on the crest of the highest knoll he saw that this pleasant new range of his was almost completely surrounded by settlements and smoky villages; but beyond these, to the north and west, ran a purple barrier of mountains, as wild-looking as his own Ringwaak. He had half a mind to set out for these mountains at once, not quite liking the girdle of civilization which he saw drawn about him. But that was only a passing whim. He had no other fault to find with his present domain. Game was